PRAISE FOR NATAI

'A tasty tale of love, in___gue and murder'
Lin Anderson

'Hilarious, brave and original. I love Natalie Jayne Clark's voice'
Helen FitzGerald

'A deft debut full of dry wit and enticing intrigue . . .
a welcome queer twist on Tartan Noir. Savour this wee
dram of mystery, mirth and murder'
D. V. Bishop

'I raced through this lively, funny, charming tale with great
pleasure, and learned a lot I didn't know about whisky too'
Ajay Close

A NOTE ON THE AUTHOR

Natalie Jayne Clark is a neurodivergent writer, editor and producer based in Perth, Scotland. Natalie writes for SNACK Magazine, is the Assistant Producer for StAnza Poetry Festival, and works across the arts and culture industry in a variety of roles. Her poetry can be found in anthologies from Flapjack Press, Speculative Books and Open Book, and she has won several poetry slams. She is also a certified whisky ambassador and is partial to a Springbank or a Bruichladdich.

THE
MALT WHISKY
MURDERS

Natalie Jayne Clark

Polygon

First published in Great Britain in 2025
by Polygon, an imprint of Birlinn Ltd.

Birlinn Ltd
West Newington House
10 Newington Road
Edinburgh
EH9 1QS

www.polygonbooks.co.uk

1

ISBN 978 1 84697 678 0
eBook ISBN 978 1 78885 716 1

LOTTERY FUNDED

The publisher acknowledges support from the National Lottery through
Creative Scotland towards the publication of this title.

British Library Cataloguing-in-Publication Data
A catalogue record for this book is available on request
from the British Library.

Typeset by Initial Typesetting Services, Edinburgh

Printed and bound by Clays Ltd, Elcograf, S.p.A.

To Mum, who taught me to read and opened up the world for me.

Eighty-one per cent of female respondents said they'd been asked the question 'do you even like whisky' while at work or while making a purchase.

— OurWhisky Foundation survey result,
July 2023

O thou, my muse! guid auld Scotch drink!
Whether thro' wimplin worms thou jink,
Or, richly brown, ream owre the brink,
In glorious faem,
Inspire me, till I lisp an' wink,
To sing thy name!

— Robert Burns, from 'Scotch Drink'

No matter how fucked up the world may get, a good dram will make it at least slightly more bearable.

— Iain Banks, *Raw Spirit*

CHAPTER 1

Eilidh

2023

My wife and I found the first dead body inside the second barrel of whisky we tested.

First, we noticed the smell. While the initial barrel had been deeply medicinal in a heady and woody sort of way, this one reeked of sharp, tart, sewagey port. Then, the colour. Instead of a rich, golden amber like the shining of a fair maiden's hair, it was goose-turd green, a shade we identified swiftly because we'd painted our downstairs bathroom the same colour after falling about laughing at the name. The final clue was the human tooth, a molar, bobbing at the top of the murky substance at the centre of the bung hole.

We rushed to decant it and prise open the barrel. Even with the liquid gone, it was still heavy. Inside was a man, skull caved in on one side, with red hair, a large wristwatch and an appalling tartan suit. Maybe it wasn't always appalling, but it certainly was now. His fingers were stiffened and curled in every direction and his body had been folded into two, and that was how he lay, at that moment, on our dusty warehouse floor.

'Eilidh, babe, what the heck?'

We were both completely naked at this point, and I didn't know what to reply, so I bent down to inspect the man more closely. She grabbed my hand before I could pull back the wet hair from his eyes.

'No, love, you don't want to be touching that!'

Her face was inscrutable, but after being together so long, I thought I could assume what was flowing through her head, that we were riding the same wave of emotions as we stared, enthralled and sickened, unable to look away from the sight before us. I don't think either of us knew how to feel.

There was no doubt that he had been murdered and hidden here, and that he made a sorry sight. There was also no doubt that he posed an awful problem to two women who had used up all their life savings, were in debt up to their eyeballs and had rabid whisky fans clamouring for updates on how their crowdfunded donations were being spent on this dilapidated whisky distillery.

After a while, she stroked my head and said firmly, 'Right, let's get these clothes back on. You grab your meds and I'll make a cafetiere of coffee, the big one. Let's check as many of these barrels as we can tonight. We don't want any nasty surprises when BBC Scotland show up.'

We'd been celebrating our purchase of this old distillery with champagne and sex, christening as much of the ramshackle buildings as it was safe to do. Afterwards, we thought it'd be fun to sample a couple of the barrels, maybe commence a bit of proper regauging, start totting up how many hundreds, or thousands, or millions, we could make from these old casks. We'd purposely started with the old ones, ones that had been there since the early seventies, ones we knew we could sell to avid whisky collectors for eye-watering sums to pay back our loans and get renovation and production started as soon as possible.

According to our records, the one containing the dead man had been left to mature since 1971, or at least there was no record of it being touched after that, and that year was confirmed through my later inspections. These days, you might move whisky from one cask to another over such a long course of maturation, so it can pull many elements of flavours from different woods and alcohols, but we'd expected a few to have been left to sit. The distillery, Ardkerran, a twenty-minute walk along the seafront from Campbeltown, had closed its doors in 1985 and been left alone ever since. These kinds are sometimes referred to as 'ghost distilleries' – not in active production, but not fully shut either. We were lucky there were even barrels left. A fifty-year-old whisky could sell for millions – a fifty-year-old whisky from an abandoned Campbeltown distillery that's matured in the same cask all that time could be priceless.

Except ours was ruined. By a man. It's not all men but it's always men, isn't it? I suppose I can't blame the man inside, but I can certainly blame the man who murdered him.

I took a double dose of my ADHD meds, smashed on our 'Angry Pop and Riot Grrrls' playlist so it echoed around the dim warehouse, and rolled up the trousers of my corduroy dungarees. I attempted to channel an aura of certainty, of resolve, to mask my thrilled horror at the dead body. I found four pens of the kind Morag favours (I knew I'd lose some in the process), three lamps from our rooms next door, two clipboards and my one very large mug that had been festering in the office upstairs.

'Right, I've brought Bruno, a big bit of caffeine and some crisps. Shall we get started?' Morag said on her way in, just as Bruno made a dash for a good sniff of the corpse.

I grabbed the dog by his collar. 'Maybe leave him outside?'

'Nah, he's been alone in the caravan for a couple of hours already. Let's just keep an eye on him. And keep him away from . . . that.'

I released our black Labrador and he stayed by my side, leaning heavily on my legs, looking up with a wide panting mouth and wagging his tail. I sighed. 'Fine. Let's divvy up the areas. Cover twice as much ground.'

I later found out that Morag had used the opportunity of grabbing coffee and our dog to be violently sick, and that every time she ducked away for a few minutes throughout the night, claiming to be topping up her coffee or nipping to the loo, she was being sick again. I had seen her watery eyes and the blotches on her face and assumed it was from exhaustion and worry, but she was simply externalising what I was feeling – that our pragmatism and prioritising ourselves over this man was wrong, that we should be calling the police immediately. But we continued.

By the time outside turned to rays of sunbeams glowing through the windows, we had tested every single barrel. We opened all the ones in the warehouses, the five in the back of the office, the few scattered behind mash tuns and inside cupboards, and even the one outside, half-buried, left as a testament that supposedly the Scots had figured out maturation before the Irish, by hiding them in the ground from the excise officers. I'd visited so many distilleries across both countries, and they all had the same story. It's an easy way to wind up men of either nationality.

And there was another body – another man – this time much thinner, but also in a tartan suit. Equally appalling. Both men were preserved in the smooth single malt. No rotting, no crumbling or blackened bits, just blood swirled with green-hued whisky and everything tainted like a ghoulish sepia filter.

The other barrels were, thankfully, simply whisky.

'Well, I suppose we could big up the ghosties for the tourists, couldn't we?'

Morag agreed. 'That's exactly what I was thinking. Imagine the merch. We could hold seance whisky-tastings . . .'

Our laughter felt hollow.

She continued: 'Do you think they've really been here since the seventies?'

'His fancy-shmancy watch stopped on the thirteenth of August 1971, so I bloody well think so.'

'Check you out, Miss Marple. Did you touch that body again?' she scolded.

I squeezed her hand. 'No touching, only looking. I swear.'

We looked at each other, knowing the topic we had to broach next. I allowed Morag, usually the more decisive of our duo, to lead the way.

'Do you . . . Should we . . . What now?' she hesitated.

We hadn't talked of it before on purpose. Instead we'd got on with the busyness of the job in hand. But I'd been mulling it over. If we called the police, who knew what they might do. Cordon it all off? Stop all renovations and production till they had 'concluded their investigations'? How long would that take?

Morag had clearly been thinking along the same lines. 'Look. Ultimately, they've been here for decades and no one has claimed them. I mean, we could do some googling ourselves but—'

'The Gannt chart.'

'The Gannt chart! Exactly. I've worked so hard on that baby. We have such a strict schedule to keep to. We have the roofers in tomorrow, well, today now, and all those people who paid into the crowdfunder hassling us on social media already, loans due any day . . . And there's all the other stuff I've put in place for us to get whisky production started up again A.S.A.P.' Morag enunciated each letter with a minister's point, a hangover from her debating days.

To be honest, I was glad she wanted to hide them too.

We'd worked so hard to pull this off and still had such a long road ahead of us.

'Right, ma'am,' I said. 'What should we do now then?'

'Put them back in their barrels, pour their fusty whisky back in with them, mark them, and then hide them among a few random ones somewhere.' She pulled off her bright, yellow-framed glasses and wiped them with purpose using her monogrammed handkerchief.

I knew we both thought our discovery was, on some levels, quite cool and deliciously dark, but although they say bold women make history, I wasn't sure I was keen on the trouble it could cause if we were discovered to have known about the bodies, and I was definitely freaking out about the camera crew coming in to document our renovations. How could we hide such a thing when they were here? I said as much, and she pulled me in for a big cuddle. Bruno came jumping up too, paws on our sides, hoping that finally he was wee enough again to be picked up.

'We'll cross that bridge when we come to it. First, roofers in an hour. Then the TV crew. Bodies later. Let's tidy up.'

A deep voice called through from the adjacent room. 'Hello? Anyone there? Is that Morag? I've been trying to find you for half an hour. Hello?'

We sprinted to the doorway the voice was coming from, just managing to stop him before he could come in. I couldn't hear what he was saying over the rushing noise in my head and I willed my eyes to be less wide. As the three of us talked he edged closer to the doorway to the warehouse, tilting, trying to look inside. One of the roofers. I kept sneaking glances down my dungarees to see if any of the stains gained from the evening's activities were suspicious or could pass as another addition to the noodle soup collection.

And so, the bodies remained, in the warehouse behind us, bent brutally at the waist, as they had been since rigor mortis set in over fifty years ago.

CHAPTER 2

You

1971

You notice the blood only after the last barrel lid has been battered down. It's run all down the mallet and pooled in the frills of your shirt.

The others will be here soon. The sun is already creating spotlights along the shelves and floor, and the seabirds outside are insinuating themselves into the morning chorus. You expect your breath to come out in frosty plumes, or maybe fiery flickers after such a cold dark act, but it's still August, still warm edges to the salt-sea winds.

First you clean; you wipe away as much of the blood as possible and grab handfuls of dirt and dust and sawdust from anywhere you can find it, soak it up, dirty up the barrels. Have them hiding in plain sight in among their brethren. You decide that later you'll roll them into the sea. They're most likely to end up on the coast of Ireland; then it's not your problem anymore. It was in the news this week – a Catholic priest killed by the British army, hundreds arrested and fleeing from their homes. The Irish aren't going to care about two dead Scots bobbing along their shores.

But now you have several buckets of whisky and no clue what to do with them. The cooper is slow and never puts together more barrels than are required, and in the hazy aftermath of the murders you chose to empty out two of the recently filled barrels and shove them in, topping up the space with the newly distilled whisky.

The cracking sound their bodies made was like cap bombs hitting cement.

CHAPTER 3

Eilidh
2023

Will the cameras pick up on my guilt? I've always been terrible at those subterfuge games our friends love so much. Mafia, Chameleon, Coup. I've always been accused of being the liar, the guilty party, even when it's not me. My face just looks that way. I'm nervous for the person who *is* in trouble, whether it's me or not, and it shows.

Even as I waited for the BBC cameraman to set up, I kept twisting and untwisting the bottom of my beige jumper, selected by Morag from her carefully curated dark academia wardrobe of browns and greys so I seem as credible as possible to appeal to the audience, like I know what I'm talking about.

And I do, really; I've been writing about whisky for years. It began at uni, at nineteen, when I was still pretending to be straight, to myself and everyone around me. The photographs of me from that time, with my fake tan and rictus smile and thick stripes of blonde highlights, make me shudder now.

I had ended up in a new pub in town, in Stirling. I was meant to be going to the library to get an essay written – I always struggled to write at home then – but the pub happened to be right next to the bus stop where I was waiting and the bus was late. Hand-painted lettering proclaimed that the pub contained over a hundred types of whisky and rum, and the thought of spending the fiver in my pocket on one of those sounded much more appealing than using it for a bus fare and sitting in the library all afternoon.

All men – the pub was already full, at 1 p.m., with just men. I recognised a couple whose usual haunts were up the road, but this was a special occasion. A new place for them to rest their bones, have real human connection beyond their telly sets. For those who had wives, it was a warm space to hide from them for a few hours.

The bartender and owner was a small lady, who used a bar stool to gain the height required to survey her one-room pub. A people pleaser, I quickly discovered she loved a woman who knew her whisky, although I later found out that she could not tolerate drunk women.

That day, I strode to the bar purposefully, pushing between the men who gathered there. They smelled of Brylcreem and rolling tobacco. Like my grandfather. Once I reached the bar, however, I was already lost. An oak archway presided over and girdled the glass shelves upon glass shelves of bottles, variegated liquids in browns and oranges and yellows.

'A . . . whisky, please.'

The men next to me, who had already been staring

at this young woman encroaching on their space, started guffawing.

Winnie saved me. 'Aye, you'll be wanting our malt of the month then. A Springbank ten-year-old. Don't mind them, they're all right really, and know they should try harder to welcome new folk.' She knew many of them from her time bartending elsewhere in the town, she told me later.

They shuffled along to give me more space at the bar, but apparently my asking for Pepsi in my drink was a step too far, and they snorted in harmony.

'Right, you have three options. You can have it neat, as they call it. As is, aye? You can add a bit of water from this.' She lifted a sturdy ceramic jug with flaked rust-orange writing, 'Don't be vague, order Haig' painted on the front. I tell you now, I was not keen on taking a drop from something that had been sitting in close proximity to these moaning, crusty, hairy-armed men all morning. 'Or, you can have an ice cube. I wouldn't have more than one, else they'll start calling you names.'

'Uh, neat, please.'

The rain smattered the windows, the men's conversations became murmurs, and it was just me and Winnie. She taught me more in that half an hour than I'd learned in my whole first year of uni. How to smell, how to taste, how to make a ritual of a mere drink. At one point, she brought a pipette from behind the bar and dropped in exactly three drops of water. She described it as 'opening' the whisky, and as the oily liquid shifted and moved in a microcosm of a hurricane, I *could* see it opening in front of my eyes, changing to something almost imperceptibly new. My English teacher had pronounced the word 'appreciate' with an 's' sound instead of a 'sh' sound and her voice came into my head. Is this the epiphany some people experience bird watching or climbing a Munro? Appreeseeate.

I came back every time my student grant money landed to try more whiskies. Suddenly the uni library seemed more appealing – they had reams on whisky and the drinks industry. I started doing things like visiting Crieff just to see Scotland's oldest working distillery and travelling to Perth to browse the local history shelves of the library to find out more about the Dewar brothers, and I once caught the meandering four-hour bus from Glasgow to Campbeltown to taste Springbank at its source.

Now, here I was, dressed in a beige sweater that wasn't mine, in Campbeltown, nearly two decades later, with a beautiful wife, proudly bisexual, my very own whisky distillery, replete with a pair of decades-old corpses, with someone asking me questions on camera for the BBC.

'You're well known in Scottish whisky circles for your long-running, successful blog "Wisdom in Whisky" and the subsequent prize-nominated book of the same name. Can you tell us more about how that began? Please remember to mention the question in your answer this time.'

'Yes. Well–'

'And to look into the camera.'

'Haha, this is why I have a blog, not a vlog.' Heather didn't laugh. I pulled the sleeves of the jumper over my hands and stretched my arms outwards, looking over to the purply water's edge, as if taking it all in before I tried again.

'I began my blog "Wisdom in Whisky" while I was still at uni, in Stirling, because it was my obsession at the time. I'd had a few before – just ask my old flatmates about my torrents of tangles of threads during my cross-stitching phase or the period where I didn't leave my room because I was watching every single Jonestown documentary.' Heather looked blank. Maybe she didn't want to hear about that. I hate people who don't show their thoughts on their faces. I can't help but do it myself, so it doesn't seem fair.

'I tried my first whisky in a new pub that opened up in 2005, in Stirling. I was led through a tasting – a private tasting, essentially – and then I saw it in a whole new light. It was like magic, how something that before simply seemed to all be the same brown liquid now came to me as layers and layers of sensory experience and care. I think it was when I first learned about maturation that I was hooked.

'The casks, the barrels, add so much depth to the liquid. I love that whatever they held before – sherry, bourbon, port, even whisky – influences the new-make whisky we put inside to mature. Not only that, the casks are toasted to break down the structure of the oak and sugars, and how lightly or heavily you toast the wood creates different flavours again. Some even say the type of soil in which the trees are grown affects the flavours. Distillers might take into account the rainfall of the area of provenance and how the wood was originally dried. That's all without taking into consideration the size of cask you use, how many times it's been used before, how long you leave your whisky in there, how many casks you move the whisky between, the weather as it matures and the geography of the area where it lies – even the way the logs were originally cut can affect the final product because of how the wood grain contacts the alcohol. And that's just one element of the process of whisky creation.'

I was still getting zilch from Heather.

'My blog though ... you asked me about that. Essentially, I wasn't going to my lectures, for a variety of reasons, and I started writing the posts for fun, instead of doing my essays. I was meant to be studying English, because that's all I was really good at, except after one of the first seminars, your classic "death of the author" one, I became more interested in philosophy. If I'd been more proactive, maybe I might have changed subject and actually finished with a decent grade, but . . .'

I'd forgotten the question. Heather prompted me: 'Yes, and tell us about the book and blog, please. How did that happen? How did you get noticed?'

'I had thought it was funny to compare a whisky to a certain philosopher or their, like, policies? No – schools of thought. So, like, an Auchentoshan to Noam Chomsky, or a Glen Livet to Hannah Arendt. It sort of caught on – it was a different way of viewing both the whisky and the philosopher, I think. It grew from there, but the real growth was when I branched out from philosophers to writers and thinkers of any kind and when the comments sections in

16

themselves began containing essays. That was a bit of a wild ride – I started getting invited to things. I got an offer from a publisher too. I had a year to write the book, but really most of it was written in the last month. Anyway, it was, I suppose, semi-successful, as successful as a book can be these days without being Richard Osman or whoever. I moved beyond the pub in Stirling and went to tastings and festivals elsewhere. Most of my student grant went on that, actually. That's how I met Morag too.'

I looked about for Morag, for some assistance, a nod that confirmed I wasn't wittering and I was making sense. But she was still dealing with the roofers, who had decided to start charging god knows how much just to survey the buildings before they even began work. I paused and glanced at my interviewer.

Heather was a few years younger than us, someone who seemed to have skipped the awkward, unsure years of her youth and zipped straight to the self-assured I-don't-smile-for-anyone phase. Morag knew her quite well from her reporting days and told me multiple times how lovely she was and not to read anything into her dour facial expressions.

'Thanks for that, Eilidh. I think we've got all we can outside for today. It's bloody miserable.'

Like she could talk.

'So how about we do some inside shots? All those barrels in the warehouse? You've not got much else to show for the cameras yet. Maybe find one with a historically significant year on it? How does that sound?'

Yesterday morning, when the roofer arrived early, very conscientious and aware of the awful windy and winding road down from Tarbet, we hadn't yet put the bodies away. It was Bruno that saved us. Big dopey lovely Bruno. He basically took a running jump onto the man and crashed into him with such force he ended up on his back. Our dog is mostly well-trained, but sometimes he gets excited, and he hadn't slept much. Neither had we. Morag had taken the roofer, Rodney, to recover with a cup of tea, far away from the warehouse. It had been up to me, alone, to cram these bodies back into their cask coffins, replace the fetid liquid and roll the barrels away.

Let's just say I hadn't yet told Morag I'd been unsuccessful in my endeavours.

CHAPTER 4

You
1971

You assist the manhunt, the search for the missing men. Of course you do – you worked with them for five years, occasionally stayed for a dram at the end of a shift, and in a town the size of Campbeltown their disappearance is big news, even if the police don't seem particularly galvanised.

As you stomp through the dark peaty fields along the single-track lane, trying to hit the mud with quick, forceful steps so as not to sink too far up your trusty wellingtons, you remember their touches. Their secret touches. You remember the twisting and grasping and gasping as the three of you tumbled over bed and floor. It had almost become routine. One of you would leave a crystal glass tumbler upside down on the lucky barrel and that would be your signal to meet. Sometimes it happened accidentally; a night of a few drinks would leave you all with buzzing skin to taste each other again.

But no more.

These wellingtons were your brother's once, and they

are a touch on the large side. Even with toes stuffed and an extra pair of socks, you slip somewhat. But they are thick and sturdy, and better than any boots you could afford.

'They can't have just disappeared like that. D'ye think they were both being stupid on the sea like last time?' Your search partner wants to talk. You sigh in response. They keep going.

''Cause you were quite close, weren't ye?'

You stop and shine your torch in his face. 'What d'ye mean?'

'Just that. I seen you three huddled at the pub a coupla times. Having a cuppa in the office. Playing darts.'

What is more believable, and advisable, to say next – that you did get along very well and knew things about each other that no one else did, or you simply connected on the matter of darts and a couple of other innocuous topics? Is the cold damp feeling on your feet a symptom of anxiety or are these wellies finally giving way?

'Aye, they've always accepted me into the group, which is nice. I suppose I feel . . . I felt . . . I got on with them, like. But, aye, who knows what could have happened to them? I don't think searching in the dark is going to do much good. Do you?'

He stops and lights a cigarette, hands it to you, then lights one for himself. 'No, I suppose you're right. You should be tucked up at home now anyway, not out here with an old man like me.'

The sky hasn't yet fully turned to night; dark periwinkle edges frill the blush streaks of clouds, but the thin crescent

20

moon is nonetheless sharp and clear. It has been two days since you killed them, and your feelings have not yet settled.

It was a heat of the moment act, certainly. But one you would do again. Your gut hasn't steered you wrong so far.

The main problem is you haven't been able to move the barrelled bodies. The first day the men didn't show up at the distillery, it was put down to a harmless hangover, even though Finola swore she hadn't seen either return to their homes, and work continued as normal. This morning was when the concern seeped in. These two were the centre of the place – the heart of the whisky, some would say, like the part of the distillate we desire most in the whisky-making process, clear and true.

If only others had seen their hearts like you did.

CHAPTER 5

Eilidh
2023

Heather's usual flat line of a mouth morphed deeper and deeper into an upside-down 'u' the more I gabbled and attempted to justify why we couldn't go into the warehouse. Unsafe for humans, rotting beams, the rats ruled there now, splinters the size of your thumb, much too damp for cameras . . . but nothing deterred her – each item just made her chin jut further forwards.

'I think we're capable of filming in such conditions, right. We were the ones who broke the story of the dodgy shortbread factory a few years back. They might not have had rats, but it was certainly unsafe. Right, boys?' The cameraman and sound guy both nodded. 'But, also, we do want to keep this lovely and light. Celebratory. I just think it would make a great "before" as well. Shall we see what Morag thinks?'

Heather's wellingtons turned sharply left, and the trio began heading straight for the warehouse.

She reminded me of Susan, a woman I met early in my

whisky journey. I still wasn't sure how I felt about Susan, but we continued to send each other voice notes or links to articles occasionally.

Susan is about fifteen years my senior, a short woman who was never without her heels, but she always kept up, set a fast pace even. I used to imagine proposing a race to her. In my mind, she always won, even in those acid green stilettos with the black plastic bows she favoured.

I never knew where I stood with Susan, then. She seemed equal parts helpful, almost maternal, and equal parts frustrated and resentful. I was twenty-one when we first met, about a year after my blog first started gaining traction, and I was being invited places, a welcome relief to my bank balance. From then on, I often had plenty of free booze and food plus my entry tickets paid for, if not my travel and a night in a hotel as well.

I think it had a lot to do with being the women in the room. I'd already experienced it a few times, that weird glittering air that seemed to surround me when in the presence of only men. I recall one whisky festival – more like a few stands of sellers in a run-down hotel ballroom than a festival – where I felt followed by the other attendees. It was like the crowd would push and swarm towards wherever I was in the room, and they kept laughing at my jokes, kept fighting to follow up my stories with one of theirs. They wanted to impress me. I was automatically the most attractive person in the room simply because I was the only one with breasts and a handbag. I was impressive to them because I was a woman who knew her whisky. If a man had been saying the same things, he would not have scintillated so much.

So when there's another woman in the room, it generally goes one of two ways: you cling to each other, whisper 'thank god' and tell each other which men's hands to watch out for; or you seem like magnets with opposing ends facing each other, circling but always keeping as much distance between you as possible, watching but never meeting eyes, unconsciously or consciously ranking each other's attractiveness and cool factor. Or at least that's what I used to do. I thought that was what women were meant to do.

I would like to have said it's changed, and it has in some ways. In 2018, the first woman was inducted into the whisky hall of fame, which was over a decade after Susan and I first met.

Susan, before I came along, was used to being the only gal in the room. She wore tight dresses and those killer heels, and no one could deny she knew her shit, more so even than a lot of the men who'd been around the block for much longer than her. No one could deny, however, that what made her stand out was her gender. The men's voices rumbled and ricocheted; Susan's voice tinkled and bounced. Then I came along, a prodigy simply because I started in the game so young, and fell so deep into what I liked to call the whisky 'lore'. I was the new shiny thing, the new *young* shiny thing, and I'll admit now I basked in it. Who doesn't want to be called beautiful? Who doesn't want to be 'just the breath of fresh air this industry needs'?

(*Whisky Magazine*, January 2007). Not only that, but I could hold myself as one of the lads.

The currency for women was changing. No longer was ascribing to femininity the thing to do: eschewing it was. I wore Converse, no makeup and a man's watch. I knew about video games and Quentin Tarantino movies. My glaring gap was always and still is sports, but I could generally nod and smile my way through those conversations.

Susan was shrewd. She'd built up a thick skin and could read these rooms of men better than me. I was initially frightened of her, and I thought her brusqueness was her disliking me as competition. That's just her demeanour, but I avoided her at these gatherings all the same.

Until, once, after a long day of nosing and tasting and my alcohol tolerance not being what I brazenly claimed it was, she saved me. Her withering look, her ice-laden tongue, her fierce grip on the man's arm as she suggested he 'call it a night now and stop being a wanker', saved me. He'd been pushing me closer and closer into the wall, his thick knuckles grabbing my hips and hands and hair, his breath pluming through my nervous laughter, and I might have actually followed him up the stairs had Susan not come and saved me. I don't think I wanted to, but I didn't want to cause a fuss either and didn't know how to get away without one.

From then on, we worked the rooms as a duo, riffing on each other, geeing ourselves up over our respective studies and neat new facts, and the way we, together, had developed an elevated figurative language to describe the aromas.

She rarely smiled though, and I came to respect that. You earned a Susan smile. She wouldn't smile just to put other people at ease or if something wasn't funny, actually.

I tried to imagine Heather as the same: someone who's done the hard graft in the media world, someone who was now seeking her own stories and writing her own scripts because she put in the work. She didn't laugh along with the tasteless jokes or simper to men. She just got the job done.

She was just trying to get her job done with us; she had a vision and she knew what would work well, and a wide shot of our warehouse, scattered with barrels and peeling paint and corroded pipes, would do very nicely. How would I have spoken to Susan in this case?

'I have an even better room to show you. The Aladdin's Cave above the bottling room.'

'Oh?'

'Apparently, a guy who worked here decades ago, who legend says was made redundant and rehired several times over the course of the whisky booms and busts, kept everything he could, and it's all in that room.'

'When you say "everything" . . .?'

'You have to see, I can't explain. It's magical, unlike anything you've ever seen.'

She lapped it up. I had found a better solution for her, an intriguing mystery to unpick. I started pacing towards the bottling room, bitterly cold wind lashing my face and hair, before she could think about it too long.

The bodies would have to wait. I just had to hope they hadn't started rotting yet.

CHAPTER 6

You
1975

You've settled into your new rhythm now. People had always pegged you as an outsider, a weirdo, maybe even a little impertinent, and you've absolutely leaned into this since the murders. You've become bolder, making declarations on the warehouse floor, putting your knowledge of people and whisky to good use, something that they should have appreciated before, ingratiating yourself successfully into all areas of the business. You've become indispensable. The beating heart of operations. They trust you now.

It's strange to live with this power. Whereas before, you kept to the sidelines, knowing your place and letting them speak, now you speak – and you bloody well speak your mind.

The quality of the whisky has undoubtedly soared from what it was three years ago.

It began really when you started visiting the lads on the nightshift. Folk regularly donder their way to the distilleries once the pubs shut, help keep the hardworking men sane, maybe pinch a nip or two.

You weren't interested in a nip – you'd never say no, naturally, but you were there for the wisdom, the little secrets passed along to a select few.

You even bought them a record player and albums, to help them pass the time. The Rolling Stones, T. Rex, 10cc, David Bowie. They loved that. They loved that you thought of them on your trip to Glasgow, loved imagining you in a record store, long fingers flicking through the selections, finding music you thought they would enjoy.

The trick is to ask the right questions, to strike the rich seam of their particular passion, in a nonchalant, curious, unthreateningly tipsy-sounding kind of way, and you're very good at it. Eric – he was the one to interrogate about cask storage, and Neil could find the heart of the whisky like no one else. Multiple times, he'd be there, waxing lyrical about *fog lifting off a loch* and *mother nature's unparalleled prowess* and really enjoying the sound of his own voice and you as his captive audience. Hugh was the one to go to, to sneak tastes from the casks, to experiment with blends, for a good bloody laugh, and more than once you two were found in a compromising position in a dark corner, whisky slopped down your fronts and on to the floor.

You began with gentle nudges, suggestions, hints, happy to plant an idea during one of your nighttime sojourns and to allow these men to present these notions as their own and take the credit for them. Then, you inserted yourself into meetings you weren't invited to. You could see the bigger picture. The seeds you sowed sprouted, and their tendrils wound their way round them, each one benefiting from your foresight, and their trust in you bloomed.

Today, three years and a day since your first spirit was casked, nearly four years after killing your ex-lovers, you are gathered to sample.

Hugh stands so close you wonder whether you'll be able to parse the whisky's aromas from his Old Spice aftershave. Part of your insertion into the distillery's inner circle all these years has been to serve your town, elevate your whisky, the lifeblood of this peninsula. In truth, part has been to find a partner in crime, of sorts. Someone you can divulge your bloody secret to, someone who can assist in the disposal of the barrels that likely wouldn't slosh but would instead thump if they were to be moved. And to steer folk away from testing and sampling and utilising those two particular sherry butts till you do so. Which, you rationalise, is also part of your service to the town.

This latter task of yours has been easier than you expected – pre-murder, you had primarily clerical tasks anyway, and now you are deferred to in many blending and bottling decisions. Those two casks, plus a few others, have been kept aside for the long haul. Your long-term thinking was applauded – retain a select few barrels to add complexity to later blends, to ensure a certain rarity and to encourage customers to ask for a particular vintage, like wine. It just so happens that two barrels have been left off the regauging checklist, and no one here is quite so dedicated or detail-oriented to notice the error.

It is you who gets to slam and screw the bung out of

this, the first of your distillates. It is you who dips the long beak of the copper valinch in. It is you who drips and spurts whisky into the glasses. It is you who observes the gathering around you and only pretends to sample. And you'd prefer to let someone else speak.

'What d'ye think?' you prompt.

'The colour . . . bit, bit more burgundy than usual. Fruity . . . very fruity.'

'Peppery. The tip of my tongue is peppery and further back I taste . . . dates–'

'Yes, dates and gingerbread.'

'Aye, a spiced fruit pudding.'

There's silence for a while, an appreciative and gluttonous one, like the opening few minutes of a family Christmas dinner.

You wonder whether it will be enough to save this distillery.

CHAPTER 7

Eilidh
2023

The Aladdin's Cave was something to behold. I still haven't found out the name of the oddball from the past who clearly had some intense hoarding habits, but none of us can deny the draw, the magnitude of *stuff* to poke and pick and keek at, a visual and very human record of history.

Zahir, the camera guy, was in his absolute element. I watched him zoom in and out, pan the camera up and down and round in circles. He kept doing this weird movement where he started high up and twisted the camera as he came down faster, closer to the items. Occasionally, he picked something up and placed it an inch along from its previous position, or turned it a few degrees to face a new angle.

On the table closest to where I was standing were crystal tumblers – their criss-cross diamonds caked with buff-coloured dust, resembling the uniformity of dry riverbeds – and boxes of nails, variegated with a spectrum of rusts, plus old cooper's tools. I assumed they were all cooper tools – they looked like them to the best of my knowledge. Before the discoveries of the other night and our panicked foray into YouTube to ascertain how best to pull apart and put back together whisky barrels, I hadn't given cooperage much thought, despite my preoccupation with casks, and how complex a skill it is to make barrels – it takes over five years of apprenticeship to master. You'd think it would be a topic I'd have fallen into by now. I added it to my notes app list of erratic interests to follow up later. Over in one corner were brooms, pipes of varying lengths, a wheel of a tractor, charred staves, desiccated paint buckets and rubber hoses. The scene was beautifully finished off by the dirt-gilded windows and their sills of mouse droppings and dead flies.

The best part, though, was undoubtedly the box Heather unearthed from underneath the battered desk which had hitherto been obfuscated by an oil-stained sheet. Behind the box was an urn of someone's ashes – a disturbing mystery for another time – but inside the battered banker's box was all manner of documents and photographs. I groaned at the thought of having to sift through hundreds of pages of handwritten reports, but the photographs hooked something in me.

Heather held and then moved each picture to the back of the pile, one by one, as we looked through the snapshots together. Some were even in colour. There was an image of the shopfront of the whisky shop in town with gold letters prominent on the bottle green paint, a collection of people outside the bowling club, someone in front of their sailing boat. There were, excitingly, a few in and around the distillery site: an array of men and two women sitting and standing in front of the wrought-iron gates; a picture of the copper stills, standing as they are now, except gleaming; a woman addressing a group of men in the warehouse, barrels as far as the eye can see.

Although I have made it my mission to uncover as much about women in the whisky industry as possible, it was not the strangeness of a woman from so long ago, clearly a leader in this situation, that was the most intriguing to me – it was the group picture, in front of the gates. When we arrived, these gates had a sign saying 'DISTILLERY CLOSED – NO VISITORS' and were distinctly more mottled and worn than in this image. I couldn't be a hundred per cent sure any of them were our casked cadavers, but in that photograph there were three men who were most definitely wearing tartan suits. I didn't want to act too excited, and I certainly didn't want Heather taking these photographs away yet, although they would definitely add a beautiful touch to her documentary about us, about our distillery.

Zahir and Gordon (the sound guy) were drawn to our oohs and aahs and woofts, and came to huddle behind us. There were more women in the photos than I expected. I know I suffer from assuming women were excluded from a lot of things, but, in my defence, they regularly are, and are often erased after the fact too. Women are represented in less than 0.5 per cent of recorded history, and even then, most of that is when they committed crimes or, more likely, were victims of crime. However, I have had women, people like Susan, tell me before that it wasn't like there were zero

33

women in the industry in the past, that, in fact, many were actually embraced by the men.

Another photo stood out. It was the woman from before, the one orating, the one who appeared to have the attention of all the men. Except she is alone, in a tartan blazer and matching skirt, arms folded, a serious look deep into the lens, and it is soft focus, a halcyon portrait of sorts. I wondered if the others saw the nervousness below the surface of her austere demeanour.

I've always avoided cameras. My friends get fed up because I hate it when they take pictures or videos without giving me advance warning, but I also only like candid photos of myself. I can hear my dad telling me so often as a child, 'Smile like you usually do,' and I always thought I was. My natural smile is quite sweet actually. My posed one is dreadful. And these days I forget I have a wee bit of a double chin, because when I look in the mirror, I tense my jaw and pull my head upwards, automatically. Cameras always seem to pick it up, whatever the angle of the photographer.

When my blog went 'viral', as they say now, the narcissist in me was thrilled with the attention, ecstatic at the invites, the press, the awards. Afterwards, though, I'd inevitably focus on the photographs – on me. So many of these places want a bio and a picture too, and I kept reusing something my old flatmate took on a night out where my makeup was heavy, I was laughing into the night sky, and I was wearing my leopard-print faux fur jacket, so I looked like a much more glamorous version of myself, the version of myself I pretended to be as a whisky aficionado. I cropped the John Player Special fag out, of course.

Lillian was the first photographer to make me feel beautiful – or whatever it is you're meant to feel at these things. At twenty-five, I'd decided I was sick of seeing the same photo of me, sometimes blown up large on a poster, and admittedly I was looking more than a little older than that teenager in the leopard-print jacket, so I booked a professional.

Semi-professional, I guess – she hadn't finished her course yet and I was only her second customer. Her photography space looked much like the Aladdin's Cave. Her studio was a small corner of a huge storage room above the Glasgow Barras and was where her dad kept his stall's stock, plus all the detritus he'd picked up over the years. Battered top hats, plastic toys from the nineties, old televisions, broken games consoles and theatre costumes seemed to be his retail drugs of choice. That suited Lillian – more props to play with.

Perhaps it was that she felt like a kindred spirit – her mind wandered too much to let her finish a thought and everything was 'groovy'. She's why I use the word 'groovy' so much now, and maybe Morag will never forgive her.

YouTube had already begun to overtake blogs by the time I went to Lillian, and although I could feel my audience slipping away from me to this shiny new media, I could not bear to film myself. My words written down are just the right amount of removed from me that I can enjoy creating content without being too critical or self-conscious.

35

'Right, get your skirt up, your arse out and sit on that telly. Trust me, once I've seen your knickers, you'll be much more natural.' She ordered this a mere five minutes into the shoot. It definitely would have felt creepy coming from a man, but from her it was side-splitting. It was weird, but it worked.

'And hold this Sega Mega Drive like a baby. Yes, that's right, and rock it like one. Now chuck it in the air and catch it. Again. Okay, pick it up off the floor if you fail to catch it. Now look more to the left. No, left. Yep. Put this wig on it. Groovy!' She removed the pressure to be sexy, to be cool, to be poised, and she allowed me to really laugh and giggle, instead of trying to hold a stiff grin and my belly in.

The woman with the tartan blazer and serious face in that photo would have had no such experience. She looked like she was most definitely tucking in her tummy, and I imagined she was clenching her pelvic floor in lieu of her gritting her teeth.

A sudden cacophonous crash happened on the other side of the room, and a man was catapulted into a heap of buckets, some of which were definitely not empty. I rushed over to help him up, but I still clocked Heather carefully sliding the pictures into her satchel out of the corner of my eye.

'Oh, hello there,' he began, patting the dust from his jumper and eyeing up the gloop now on his trousers. 'I hope I'm not interrupting anything, I just wanted to welcome you to the area.'

By the way he was eyeing up me, the others and the

room, he was our first local on an information-gathering run. I've met the type before.

We didn't initially reply. I'd been consciously trying not to people-please or give out fake pleasantries and this man was definitely interrupting. Quite presumptuous to let himself through closed gates that proclaimed 'NO VISITORS', through the bottling room, into the back, up the stairs, down the corridor – and into this room. I jolted as I remembered what was still on the warehouse floor and attempted to change my frosty facade. I affected my nicest phone-speaking voice and dealt out some pleasantries after all.

'Thank you, that is so kind of you. May I ask, did you come straight up here? How did you know we were here?'

'Aye, I could see the shadows from outside those manky windows. That lassie with the clipboard said I could have a look round. I used to work here, you see.'

His relaxed temperament, and the fact that he sought us out at all rather than running straight to the police, helped my heart settle somewhat. He can't have been in the warehouse.

I looked over at Heather, and she might have even been smiling. Her hands were jittering in a way mine do sometimes when I see a seagull steal a whole battered sausage.

'Can you look at these photos with us? Maybe you'll recognise some people or places. Sorry, what was your name? I'm Heather, and this is Zahir and Gordon. We're here filming for the BBC.' Her polite voice was even better than mine.

'I'm John, but they call me Links or Linksy, on account of my high handicap out on the courses. Golf, I mean. And who're you?'

'Me? I'm Eilidh. A pleasure.' We moved to shake hands, and I braced to give as firm a one as I could manage (I've had a lot of practice over the years and enjoy surprising men with my grip strength), but we pulled away a millimetre before our hands connected. The gloop was all over his right hand. We laughed and shook lefts instead.

'So you'll be one of they lesbians that's bought the distillery then?'

'Um, yep, that's me.'

'Aye.' He appraised me again, then stepped around the messy newspaper pile to move next to Heather. 'Show me those photos, then.'

We had a surprisingly enjoyable hour. Heather clicked on her Dictaphone and I scrawled in my notebook, taking down as much as I could of what he told us. A large portion of it was gossip ('Oh, of course, he was having it off with the boss's missus. Dead now.'), comments on whether or not the women had let themselves go now or were known nags, reminisces about his childhood here in Campbeltown ('Did us no harm, did it?'), and an astonishing amount could be linked to various games of golf he'd played over the years.

Unfortunately, many of the identities of the subjects were unknown, but he did help us illuminate a good number. The woman in the tartan skirt, he scratched his head over for a while. Literally. Little flakes fluttered down from his hairline as he pondered. 'Aye, I know I knew her . . . but . . . haven't seen her in years. I'll ask around for you.'

Very few pictures had pencil markings on the back with the year or event, and of those most didn't have names on. I attempted to bring it back to the three men in the tartan suits.

'What about them? They look like the kind of guys who'd stand out in a crowd, no?'

He paused. Gordon had wandered off a while before and was attempting to fix something on the table in the corner – or maybe he was just playing with the tools. Zahir was filming our hands over the photos. Not a media moment to be wasted.

I scrutinised Linksy's face. Was he playing dumb? If I had murdered and barrelled two men and left them here decades ago, I'd certainly want to check up on the new owners as soon as possible, and he was the first one on the scene. Did he really know or not know some of these people? A false trail . . .

'That one seems familiar, but, no, I couldn't tell you. And a lot of folk wore tartan suits then. Not all the time, mind you. He probably wasn't a hands-on kind of guy – you know, none of them probably were, like, not a cooper or anything. Their hands look mighty clean and you can see, even though it's picture day, a lot of the others are wearing their bunnets and pinnies.'

He was right. That perhaps narrowed down my search – people who dealt with the business or distilling side, most likely.

'Oh, I know that guy!'

'Who, who?'

'That's Donald's dad – can't mind his name. Donald runs a local pub, the Drookit Dug. Best macaroni and chips around.'

He pointed at one of the three men in the tartan suits. One was tall and lanky, like the second body we found, and one had a large wristwatch and moustache, like the first body. It was the third man who Linksy was pointing at. I felt a skip in my stomach. I felt the bearded man had a secret. I felt that he was telling me he had something to do with these other two men. I felt it was divine providence that the place we were filming my very first Campbeltown whisky tasting happened to be the Drookit Dug in just a few short nights. Or was it something orchestrated by this man and his son when they invited me back in July to host there?

'So what is it you did, while you were here?' Heather was clearly keen to move the conversation on, and I probably had a bit of a glaikit look on my face as I pondered the new information being presented to me.

He lit up, puffed out his chest. 'I was the last cooper apprentice before this place shut down in the eighties. Aye, the dunnage warehouse and cooperage was my kingdom. Don't suppose I could take a look?'

Another person to steer away from that bloody warehouse.

Thankfully, evening was drawing near, and I was able to convince everyone to end the day, to go get their tea and leave me and Morag in peace to have ours. Nothing motivates like food and the way it keeps time in our lives.

I strode purposefully to the gates, the other four trailing behind me.

'Could I just . . . quickly?'

'No, Linksy, sorry. I'm bloody starving and Morag's been up since half five today . . . Wait.' I stopped to write my number in my notebook and tore the corner out and handed it to him. 'Well, it's been lovely to meet you. You're welcome to visit and of course we want to hear more, but please call first next time.'

He had the grace to look a little sheepish. 'Aye, aye . . . of course.'

'We must meet early tomorrow to plan these last few days here because we aren't back till November after that,' interjected Heather.

'And we must have time with you and Morag together, now, at these early stages.' Poor Morag hadn't factored time spent with the BBC crew into her Gantt chart. I was going to have to be the one to break it to her. At least Bruno would be there to soften the blow.

We agreed to meet at 7.30 a.m., on the dot, at the doors to the bottling room, and as soon as she took her first step through the gate and off the property I remembered.

'Heather – you've still got those photos, aye? I'd like to keep them onsite, if possible.' Plausible enough, not much to argue with there.

'Oh, right.' I think I covered my joy and relief as she reached into her satchel where she'd slipped them away again and passed the wodge over to me. 'You know, tomorrow we can have a look at the documents too. I know they're not as exciting, but some names might crop up we can explore.'

And away they went. I thought I'd have to drag Morag away from her phone calls and discussions with builders, but as soon as I drew near, I saw how tired she was, and she finished her day willingly. The builders appeared to have left early, anyway.

'We're beholden to them, Eilidh! They know there's no one else we can get on this damned peninsula!' We held each other for a while and finished with a big rib squeeze.

'No more Mrs Nicey Pants tomorrow then, Morag. You've gotta be a tough cookie, right from the start. Put on your red-framed glasses; they always make you feel a bit powerful, don't they?' I squeezed her hips. 'Plus, don't forget about *the Gantt chart*!'

She shouted, 'The Gantt chart!' at the same time as me, and it made me all the more grateful for her, for us. We ground each other. We bring perspective to everything. It's us against the world, and no matter how big or horrible things feel, we always get to end the day in bed together, cuddled up with me telling her about whichever Wikipedia or Reddit rabbit hole I ended up in that day, and her regaling me with tales and scandals from her real life or her X/Twitter life. In just a couple of days, our lives had already changed so much.

We'd spent nearly a decade in our Edinburgh flat together, both writing, both equally enamoured and jaded with the creative world. She was the editor of a column in *The Scotsman*, and wrote freelance articles for a range of papers and magazines, supplemented with random research and transcription jobs and a lovely cheque from her parents now and then. I kept up my blog weekly, religiously, and any other bits of writing and travelling I could do in my designated 'woman in whisky' niche. We went to open mics and nights out when we could, of course, but a day is only so long. We were excited by this new chapter – away from the city, away from pretentious people, away from whatever boxes we had been forced to fit into before. Once all of the crowdfunding and loans and papers were signed for Ardkerran Distillery, we sold our flat and bought a wee caravan and made the five-hour journey to Campbeltown, us and our dog.

We were going to do something real and tangible and meaningful. And we were going to do it together.

That night, we decided on dinner in bed and an adult lie-in. We were cosied up with Bruno, with *Deadloch* on the laptop, snuggling in our wee caravan pitched in the distillery yard. It was all so peaceful until I felt the jolt run through me.

I had forgotten about the bodies.

'Uhm, honey, darling, sugar pie.'

'Yes? What do you want?'

'We need to get changed back into our messy dungarees–'

'And go out in that howling wind? It's bad enough in this plastic contraption. What the heck for?'

She was not pleased, not pleased at all, but to be fair

both of us had underestimated the difficulty of getting the bodies *back in* their barrels and it was too much for just me. We left Bruno in the caravan this time. I brought the photograph of the be-tartaned men to compare.

The warehouse, unsurprisingly, was *stinking*. It was a wonder no one was drawn there by the smell. Morag was as excited as me about the photograph, or, at least, initially acted like it at the time. Although it was hard to be sure because the men were so much younger in the photograph, when we held them against the faces of the corpses, they seemed to us to match. Well, more to me; Morag could only look for a second before she turned her whole body away from them.

When I looked at the third man in the photograph again, his eyes seemed to be telling me something. Was it the illusion of the curled-up moustache over his beard, or was he smirking?

After we bashed the iron hoops back on the barrels and bleached the floor – Morag trying her best to look anywhere except at the task at hand – we used the dirt and dust and sawdust to mess them up a bit, then rolled them towards the dark corner of the dunnage where they had resided for the last five decades.

As we walked away, Morag stopped me.

'Babe, I don't think we should do anything with them again, for at least a year.' I tilted my head in response. Her hand that gripped mine was trembling.

'I mean, we don't know how safe this is. We don't know who knows. I know we laughed before, but now . . . maybe it was seeing them again. It feels too real. Too gross. Too macabre. Please, promise me – like we agreed – we keep this secret? At least until we can get whisky production going . . . at least until then.'

I held her close, wrapping my arms around her and pulling her head onto my chest. 'Of course, darling, of course.' Just then, I couldn't think of a time where I'd seen her so on the edge of tears.

But my brain . . . my brain wouldn't let me forget those men.

Who did this all those years ago? Could it have been just one person who managed such a feat? And why? What did those men do to deserve such a thing? As they say, you don't get that for nothing.

I fell asleep clutching the photograph.

CHAPTER 8

You
1979

It's your thirtieth birthday. Past your prime, some might say, but you'd never wanted to settle down anyway. The distillery is your family, your child, your awkward needy cousin or difficult senile grandfather – how you view it changes daily. It's hanging on, fingertips ripped and filled with splinters. Where you succeeded in shifting the craft of the product upwards, you have failed in the marketing. Their goodwill and belief in you only went so far, and your notions of altering the labels or updating the adverts have been spurned. Vehemently. They have a single customer in mind – a man. Older, distinguished and callus-handed, sitting down to a familiar dram after a hard day's work – or more likely a gentle day's hunting, fishing or golfing. You'll do more research. You'll convince them.

You've been gifted a golf game for your birthday from the new apprentice, Linksy – he's always trying to get in your favour somehow, and it's flattering to know that. The food at the clubhouse *is* delicious, and they do make an exception for you to join them in there for lunch sometimes. So you wear a borrowed glove on your left hand and brush off your father's old clubs. You remember your mother crocheting him the covers and can't help but stretch out the purple patterned one for the 5-wood to poke your fingers through the holes, like you did as a child.

It is a perfect day for a game, and you thank your mother for being so firm that your father take you and your older brothers out with him on a Saturday so she could 'do the laundry' in peace. Really, she was taking the opportunity to read and nap and all the things she couldn't do with three boisterous and curious weans. He taught you how to taste the wind, feel the grass's soul through your feet and up your legs to your heart, how to keep your body taut and stance solid, how to block everything else out.

How to score just the right amount, so your fellow players wouldn't get angry with you.

Although, to be fair, you have played so little since your dad finally lost the sight in both his eyes to cataracts that you're liable to fluff a few shots anyway.

Golf isn't about the game. Not really. Anyone can tell that even from what the commentators choose to include in their ramblings – a tree falling in the middle of a game or a squirrel dancing on the green is liable to be given more airtime than a cracking shot.

No, it's about being outside. It's about talking, without having to look someone in the face and calculate how much eye contact is the right amount. Or about not talking, not having to talk, and just walking and being in the company of others.

Choosing a club feels like choosing a whisky. Each one has a story, or many stories, to tell: each one elevating a particular experience, depending on the mood, the length of the day, the company. Maybe the 6-iron is the trusty one who's got you out of scrapes before – helped you escape the bunkers in a way no other one ever has, even better than your sand iron. It helps you recall games together: 'Mind that time when . . .' or 'I'll never forget . . .'

Today you've brought a Bowmore whisky in your flask, all coastal and ash, for nips to help you calculate your shots and to pass around. Nothing brings people together like the warmth of shared victuals, especially if sharing from the same vessel, in this case the pewter flask that your father never uses anymore. You trace the engraved initials with your thumbnail for good luck.

Linksy is on top form, to be fair. He's quite charming because he's so utterly himself. He's oblivious to others. He takes over the conversation, barely lets anyone finish a story, always has a tale to one up whoever is speaking. It suits you anyway; it means you can nod and listen. So much of your time is spent convincing others to listen to you, it makes a nice change to be able to sit back and allow someone else to be at the centre. The way his eyes don't quite line up – his left eye goes a little lazy sometimes, especially after a few drams – draws you to his face.

Coming across to Machrihanish, or Mach, is always an experience. It's the pockets of wealth displayed in the houses, the golf clubhouse, the cars. Your dad enjoys regaling you with the tale of when the train connecting this place to Campbeltown shut in 1933 – when coal lost its crown as king. Another Campbeltown industry dead.

You're encouraged to go first, but delicately decline the offer of a closer starting tee-off. You're hopeful, for just a moment, before an unseen hand seemingly plucks the ball from the air, whisks it sharply left and bounces it behind one of the multitudes of wee bumps in the landscape. At least it didn't take it the other way, towards the foaming beach.

Everyone whistles at your misfortune, and you take a sip from your flask while the other three take their shots. They don't fare much better, and the balls all land scattered everywhere except the long stretch of intended green.

No matter, because the salt winds batter the clouds too, turning them tumbling through shades of violet and blue, and there's nowhere you'd rather be than between the sky, sand and sea.

By the ninth hole, though, the warmth and protection of the clubhouse seem very tempting, and your Bowmore is nearly dry – but you will not be the first one to suggest retiring. You will plough on till the bitter end if you have to.

And you do – you all go another two whole hours of difficult golf, with the hills peering down in the distance. It makes the first dram inside all the sweeter, and everyone follows you in ordering a pot of tea too.

You almost feel like one of them.

You almost forget what you did to those men.

You remember how they were once ostracised too. How they were never invited to games of golf. How the search for them when they disappeared was pitiful at best. How quickly they were replaced and forgotten. How people like Linksy never even met them, only know Ardkerran without them.

But then for the second round you all order an Ardkerran, one of the newer bottlings, one that those two never had a hand in, and it is delicious and sharp, and you remember it was all worth it. Besides, you've got away with it for this long – and you allow yourself to relax a little bit more into this moment.

CHAPTER 9

Eilidh

2023

'The legs . . . they're quite heavy.'

The room murmured in agreement as they swirled their amber-filled glasses.

It had been just a few short days since we placed the bodies back in their whisky graves, and the last day the BBC team would be here for a couple of months. It had been a strain on us, but throughout we had each other, Morag and me, as it had been for over a decade. At the end of each day, no matter what the day had held, we held each other. We said good night, we rubbed our cold feet on each other's legs and we rubbed the spot on Bruno's head just above his eyes that he likes before he goes to sleep. I didn't appreciate what we had enough.

I'd been keen to do a whisky tasting early on, knew it was an excellent way to let the locals ogle us, assess how much we wanted to be part of their world. Plus, it became a way for *me* to appraise them, see them, see who chose to turn up to Ardkerran's first foray into the world in almost four decades. And since Linksy had made the connection between the third man in the photograph and this pub, a way for me to find out more about that man.

I knew I had the room hooked within the first few minutes, although admittedly the crackling fire, the candle-light dancing on the wooden walls and the rain beating the Gothic lozenge windows were doing a lot of the heavy lifting for me.

There were five full tables of folk – one made up of visiting Canadians who claimed some heritage with the place, one table who brought the average age down by at least thirty years, all dyed stripes and rainbow laces, and the rest a collection of over-fifties, some quirkier-looking than others.

The Drookit Dug means the Drunk Dog, or, if literally translated, the Damp Dog, but it really means drunk. It was just the right mix of old and new, warm and weird, worn and welcoming.

I always start a tasting with, well, tasting – sampling the first dram. The quickest way to turn a crowd nasty is to spend the first twenty or more minutes giving context or going on about yourself and why you're an expert, don't you know, while they watch the condensation run down the sides of their glasses, licking their lips as if this booze is the only thing standing between them and certain death by dehydration.

'You can almost see the fat teardrops holding fast onto the glass. They run slowly, almost not at all, down the sides. In many ways, tasting whisky and tasting wine are the same.

Whisky is accused of lacking the delicacy of wine. But we have the same intricate stages, the same intense sensory appreciation, plus I would argue much more goes into the process of making whisky and that sort of seeking of balance. Whisky is tainted as masculine. Smoky, bearded, a dark spirit. I see it as alchemy, as a witch's potion, where every incantation, every ingredient, is essential to ensure the spell works. It was women's work first, distilling and managing cellars being part of the household jobs.'

The five other women in the room nod at that. Despite women making up fifty per cent of whisky drinkers in the UK, nothing is marketed towards them, although perhaps we should be grateful because marketing to women is liable to be pandering pink and glitter and sold in sets with candles or bath bombs. I have never been to a tasting at which more than a quarter of the room have been women, and by my calculations I've been to hundreds.

At this tasting, there was me and Morag, her face still pink from the biting wind outside, and one younger woman with bright blue hair, and two older women, so diverse from each other in every way except their age. I tried to stay focused on what I had to say, but my brain was trying to pull me towards assessing everyone in the room.

'Next is the nosing. Before you nose, please know you don't have to put your hale neb – your whole nose – in. Like a good kiss, lean in most of the way, then let your lover come the final ten per cent. Right, give it a go. I don't even want you to look at your tasting cards yet, just think of memories. A walk in a forest after the rain. Your mother feeding you medicine and soup. The fire, here, that most of you have sat beside before – recall a time you spent next to it with friends. Remember a dram you've had after a round of golf or during a luscious day of reading. What scents come to you? What textures?'

If you've never been to a tasting before, you don't know that the magic comes with sharing. The flavours and aromas of the drink change as people add to the metaphorical whiteboard of ideas. I started them off.

'I get . . . have you ever toasted seeds or chopped nuts before adding them to something? It's something like that, just as they are starting to scorch. Maybe some . . .' I sniffed again. 'Cheesecake. Vanilla cheesecake. What about you?'

Silence. Teacher mode activated.

'You? What is happening for you?' I gestured my glass towards one of the older women, sharply dressed, matching earrings and necklace set, mahogany red nails, someone who treats every event as an occasion. I tried to imagine her in a bobbly fleece on a muddy dog walk, but I couldn't.

Her hair was cut in a straight edge, dyed red, flicking at the ends under her ears. She looked around sedately at the present company before she spoke. The whisky in her hand wobbled as she raised it up – from age or nervousness?

'A jam tart,' she replied assuredly.

'Think back to all the jam tarts you've had in your life. Does one stand out to you?' This garnered some titters from the group, but she was actually ready with an answer.

'My grandmother, she'd make pastry and would fill old

Schweppes lemonade bottles with water or rice, and my cousins and I would use them to roll it out. We'd use mugs to cut out the circles and spoon jam into the middle and curl it up with our wee hands. Blackberry jam – we'd pick the fruit together and she'd make it.'

A powerful memory – and it's clear the group agreed, because they started spilling over one another to share their own olfactory-layered tales: being in their father's garage and helping punch leather or woodturning on a lathe; digging for carrots in sweet soil; inhaling a well-used Bible, gifted for receiving top marks in a test at school; getting stuck up Killelan Hill as fog rolled in, passing round nips of whisky for warmth; and so many more. And we were just at the nosing.

Morag caught my eye and grinned. I almost blushed, I think. In that instant, she looked startlingly gorgeous.

And it was the first time I'd seen Heather smile. A big deep smile that pushed her cheeks to her ears. I felt the warmth of pride, like she was the teacher and I was her difficult pupil who had finally got an answer right. I felt like she had been waiting for me to show her that I could reach my potential, and this moment was it, better than all the whisky knowledge I had rattled off to her before.

Zahir had the night off so Gordon was wielding the camera for this one. I hoped he was getting all of this. Although I still suspected several of the patrons were here for a) a chance to get on the telly, or b) an opportunity to see 'one of those lesbians who's bought the distillery' up close, they did seem to be enjoying themselves.

'Now for a sip. Take the smallest sip, and hold it in your mouth for three seconds, then let it roll down the throat. Don't share anything with each other yet – enjoy this moment to yourself. Do this two more times. Write something down. When you're ready, speak to each other.'

They followed me dutifully. This was perhaps where my comparison to a teacher ends – they've never had such attentive students.

I walked around, listening to each table, inserting myself if there was a lull in their comparisons of flavours. Really, I was sussing them out, learning their names, gauging their amenability to us, these new arrivals in town, and all we represented. I tried to affix names and faces to the photographs we'd found, but none seem to fit.

Sheena was the name of the older woman with the impeccable outfit and hair and nails. Almost straight away, she offered to help us in any way she could – she was semi-retired now and would love to spend more time doing something useful and different. The other older woman, wearing a cosy, definitely hand-knitted green cardigan and perfectly round glasses while sporting a brilliant white perm, her name was easy to remember because it seemed to fit her so well: Bunty. She'd even been taking notes as I spoke which pleased me no end. She followed up Sheena's offer with one of her own, and although I should have felt grateful, I had a hard stone of fear in me too – how sensible would it be to have relative strangers in a place we knew was a crime scene? I made a particular point of storing the women's names to my memory bank.

What brought them both here that night? Again, I was aware of my misandrist assumptions, but women of their age, especially in a rural place like this, were likely to have experienced first-hand the notion that there's only a *certain kind of woman* who drinks a spirit. Even now, the chances are quite high for a woman, who is sat happily enjoying a whisky, to be asked by a man, 'Do women even like whisky?'

It was one of the first things that drew me to learning so much about whisky – a man's drink, a man's industry. There's nothing quite as delicious as the look on a guy's face when you know more about a topic than he does.

And, compared to my first whisky tasting well over a decade ago, this was a dream. I took a moment to enjoy how far I'd come, to wave back at a younger me, looking at this woman I am now.

I've always been a paradox – I love listening to strangers but hate meeting new people. I prefer alone time but dislike my own company. I adore learning and nothing brings me greater joy than sharing my latest trove of facts, but I detest talking in public and being perceived. It's become easier as time has gone on, the nerves dulled, the speech-giving grown to become part of the everyday.

Winnie got me through that first tasting back in 2009. I'd been visiting her pub for several years by that point, I was becoming more well-known in the whisky circles, and it was she who put me up to it. She made a platter of oatcakes, cheeses and grapes, cleaned out all of the ceramic water jugs (at my request – and I helped her to ensure she used scalding hot water) and printed out handmade flyers and distributed them to her patrons. I earned a tenner per person who came along, and she kept the rest, so I left with fifty pounds in total that night. Not bad for a night's work, although of course I spent days and days beforehand researching and rehearsing. None of the men sat at the same table as each other, as if they were frightened that even sitting next to each other would indicate they had feelings or, god forbid, actually liked each other.

So there I was, five men at five separate tables, unable to connect my loudly whirring laptop to the projector because I didn't have the right cable, and five whiskies to lead them through, without my meticulous PowerPoint to back me up.

In that moment, Winnie reminded me that it's not about the whisky – it's about the stories. As I was stammering through the introduction, the men clearly impatient to reach the tasting portion of the evening – some already ahead of me and blatantly drinking great gulps of it as if to remind me they knew more than me and they would do what they liked – Winnie stopped me and asked me to remind her of that story of the fire in Dundee, of the barrels rolling down the streets into the Tay. Slowly, the men put down their glasses, interjected with their own tales, and it became less about the tasting notes and more about the connection. I think I even managed to encourage them to sit closer together over two tables.

And I never tried to use a PowerPoint again, although I have been to many where they do use them. It works for some people, but not for me. I regularly record myself talking about the whiskies beforehand, listen to myself and make notes to refer to, but otherwise it's just me and the whisky doing the talking up there.

I was pretending there was no one filming there in the Drookit Dug, which seemed to be helping my camera-shy tendencies. I knew they had some good footage, and I hoped that they'd keep in the bit where I asked Sheena to be the first to share. It's all too common at events – whether they be whisky tastings or author Q&As or expert panels – for men to do all the talking. It's not always their fault, although they can be prone to delivering a series of statements or a portion of their life story rather than a question and, to be fair, women can be guilty of this too. It's often that men are the ones who put their hands up, who freely offer their ideas, and it's them who are selected by the unpaid volunteer with the roving mic. Women are too good at staying silent. I like to think I'm doing my bit to counter all this, in a very small way.

The men shared too, and all of their tales and tastes were as funny and sweet as the women's. There was a guy called Rob, or maybe Bob, who used to be a fisherman here, and could remember when Campbeltown Loch was full of fishing boats. There were a couple of local farmers, Gregor and Eddie, cousins and team captains of their respective bowling teams and darts teams. If it wasn't one, it was the other telling a raucous story to their table. One of them had been headbutted so hard by a sheep one day that it cracked his leg in half. His phone had no signal, and he couldn't move. He kept waving at passing traffic, but no one stopped – they all cheered and waved back, probably thinking how quaint and lovely this place was where farmers waved at you from their fields. He had a wee flask of whisky though, to get him through the hours before someone realised he hadn't returned home on time.

I couldn't tell how old they were, but both seemed to be trying to impress me and gather me over to their group throughout the night. Was it friendliness or something else? Linksy was there too, but stonier faced than when we last met. Was he feeling a bit ashamed of the way he'd let himself in, or was it something more insidious, something he was feeling towards me? And the Canadians just seemed happy to be there.

The rest of the tasting went amiably enough, and I knew I had definitely won over Donald, which I won't pretend wasn't an aim of mine. Once the majority had filtered out, we sat at the bar, and he told me and Morag it was the busiest the place had been in a while – what with more and more people moving away, the auld yins dying off at an exponential rate and a general lack of funds these days, fewer folk were choosing the pub as the place they spent their evenings. Unless they come for the warmth, in which case they nurse a single guest ale for an hour or more anyhow. I promised him I'd host more sessions, but attempted to temper his expectations.

'They were here partly because I'm new,' I said. 'They wanted to gawk at me, see if I was up to snuff.'

'Aye, you'll be right there, but y'know you've caused a

lot of excitement in this wee toon. That distillery employed sixty people back in the day. That's a lot for round here. You were fantastic, very knowledgeable, like. You remind me of my old dad. I mean, in terms of your knowledge, not the haircut – although you're not far off.'

I felt an affinity with him already, not just because he had that lovely mix of awkward and bold jokes, but because I could tell he was a dog owner from the pale hairs creating a constellation on his black fleece. And as Morag told me later – she always knows me better than I do myself – he was just my type in men: older, cuddly, and someone who spoke to women the same as he spoke to men. I later reinterpreted some of his winks and smiles as flirtatious, rather than sleekit.

As the fire died down, I allowed the others to do the talking. I mulled over who I had met that night and saw each photograph rise to meet me as if bobbing out of dark water, and I thought about who might be who.

None of the names matched those that Linksy could remember, and I didn't have much else to go on. He did keep pausing at the woman, but he just couldn't remember her name.

Perhaps the documents we'd found could illuminate us as to the workers in front of the gates, the be-tartaned men – and that woman in her tartan skirt and serious expression: who was she? I vowed that would be what I would do during my first coffee of the morning, before the work began for the day, while hopefully escaping the notice of my darling wife.

It was the end of August, and by November when Heather and her crew returned, we'd hoped to have all buildings cleared out, fully roofed and painted, our two copper stills cleaned and resoldered, and plenty of new pipes to play with.

Except the next morning came with an injunction.

CHAPTER 10

You

1982

They all completely tear your pitch to shreds. Completely. Entirely. Even the folk you've been working with, consulting with, do not have one good thing to say about it. Maybe they were just humouring you before. Except Hugh – lovely, dependable and weird Hugh.

'Well, I think there's a certain . . . that's to say, some people might like it. I've seen something like that on the telly, I think.'

'But it is not us, not Ardkerran. It's, it's, it's foul is what it is.'

'Un-Christian.' This gets a few nods and 'mmhmms'.

You would think you'd featured actual knobs on it or bare hairy arse cracks. All you've done is present a board with branding palettes beyond the usual dark-hued greens and browns and blues, and images of potential consumers, considering there might be a market with younger people who go out to the disco or what have you. Men who wear earrings. Women who wear trousers. You wonder which they find more abhorrent.

You hear them recite the same thing they've said a million times before.

'We have a brand. The choices are men fishing or hunting or golfing. The settings are fireside armchairs or heather-covered hills. Or nothing except letting the name speak for itself. We have sold whisky in this region for nearly a hundred and fifty years and we haven't changed a thing about that process. That's what people like about us.'

'Except . . .' you try.

'Except what? And cover that thing up.'

'We *have* changed the process. In the last ten years, we have changed where we source our barley, we've altered our maturation process. I know it's not much, but–'

'Well, we've got to keep with the times.'

The irony is completely lost on them.

'I just think–'

'Jings, crivvens, here we go again.'

'You've been happy to take my ideas before.' You're angry now, but you don't raise your voice, even though you want to.

'That's different. You've been, well, you've proven yourself to be dependable. A good neb. We only agreed to listen because of what you've given to the company!'

'Are you serious?' You might be shouting now, but only because they started it.

'Calm down!' another one of them interjects.

Calm down? Calm down? Now you are positively apoplectic. Nothing is guaranteed to make you lose your

64

rag quicker than being told to *calm down*. You know it is a fault of yours – no, wait, it bloody well isn't. You don't see others getting told to calm down around here as often as you do.

You grit your teeth and breathe your diaphragm out and flare your ribs, slowly exhaling through your nose, as quietly as you can.

'Okay,' you start. 'Please can I explain a little bit? We can put the pictures away – disregard them.'

No one stops you, so you go ahead.

'Right, I understand the classic and traditional connotations whisky has. *Our* whisky has. I think I know what you're worried about – that if we try to expand our market beyond these older gentlemen,' you hopefully conceal a wince at the phrase, 'that they will no longer buy from our distillery because we will have tainted ourselves in their eyes. And, yes, they are dependable. We have a solid customer base that always buys two for themselves or for their grandads for Christmas and maybe one for a birthday. But what if we could sell to clubs? Bars? In one night alone, a club in Glasgow could get through several of our bottles. You can't deny our sales are way down – our old faithful customers are literally *dying off*! We're up against vodka, more is being done with rum. Plus, women–'

They cut you off.

Between them, they give a list of counterarguments: we have stayed in business when all but two other Campbeltown distilleries have closed down precisely because we have stayed the same; our whisky has heritage; whisky isn't made to be mixed; whisky is premium and superior to all these other spirits; whisky is a product of Scotland, a noble country of inventors and dour, sensible faces. You just wish more of them left this peninsula now and then, then they'd see they are in their own tiny, awful bubble.

They don't want to hear about your research from London, from America, from Japan, from Glasgow or Edinburgh or Dublin. They don't want to hear what other distilleries are doing. The Ardkerran label, the logo, hasn't changed since 1888, and they aren't about to be the ones to change it.

You watch the head distiller take his stupid notes in his ridiculous slanting handwriting. You watch the shaking heads, the averted eyes, the crust flaking from Boris's knuckles as he scratches them firmly.

Why can't they see what you see? You take one final punt: 'Sales are down from last year by nearly twelve per cent. They are down twenty per cent from what they were three years ago. No fewer than thirty distilleries have shut across Scotland in the last five years. You can't keep your heads in the sand. The industry is in trouble. *We* are in trouble.'

But they won't have it. This is the way things have always been done, so that's how they'll keep doing them. How much longer will they have faith in the old ways of doing things?

'I'll admit it's concerning. Aye, no doubt, but come on now, why don't you sit down, and we can talk through other strategies. You can stay, if you like.' His patronising, faux-soothing voice and hand on your back is almost as infuriating as being told to calm down. But you do – you sit down. You bite your tongue. You don't offer suggestions or try to butt in unless they directly address you – which they don't, except for at the end when they ask: 'Any more clever ideas from you?'

'Well, if we could go back to the whisky ambassador idea. I know traditionally we've had men go out to America and Central Europe mainly. But what about if I . . . well, what if I went? Somewhere else? To Asia?'

They could fire you, of course they could. But you are still too valuable to them. They ask you to leave the room while they discuss, but when you go back in, even though their faces are taut, you know they have agreed to your suggestion.

Not before they have suggestions of their own, regarding how you should dress and how you should protect yourself, how you should present Ardkerran of course.

You celebrate, with Hugh and his wife, after. An arrangement that has been informal and infrequent, but at least a few times a year since a particularly messy Hogmanay party four years ago. Their kids are upstairs in bed. A light dinner, at least one bottle of wine per person, perhaps a nip or two of whisky, and then the rest of the evening spent in all kinds of ways with all kinds of moans in the guest bedroom on their ground floor. You always make sure to go home before either of them wakes up.

CHAPTER 11

Eilidh
2023

In Scotland, they call an injunction an interdict, owing to the quirks of Scots law, but they amount to the same thing – notice to 'stop harmful activities'. We were to appear in court in December, when we could attempt to appeal or else it would stick. In the meantime, we were blocked from renovating certain buildings and had to allow anyone sent by the opposing party to gather evidence free rein of the distillery. It was issued by some group who used the name 'Campbeltown Cares' as a front. We'd barely begun rebuilding, and already SEPA – the Scottish Environmental Protection Agency – was on our doorstep to begin the process.

Two of them arrived, black satchels filled with testing equipment and a plethora of tuts and tsks to boot. They listed a litany of potential issues. Pollution of local waterways, disruptive smells, incorrectly disposed waste – apparently there were even sandpipers that regularly nest in one of the buildings.

'Aye, usually they'll nest elsewhere on their migrations, but they're known to favour drier areas more than most shorebirds. And these wee peeps have picked your place to do it.'

I attempted to radiate calm to settle Morag's poorly disguised apoplexy. Not only did we have to send the contractors home at 11 a.m. with a full day's pay, but we would have to reserve repairs to only three of the eleven buildings for the foreseeable future. Not good for the goose or the Gantt.

I pulled her inside our caravan at the edge of the grounds for a quiet moment alone. As we waited for the burbling kettle on the small gas stove to reach boiling, I firmly squashed her arms into her sides to halt her pacing. She made a cute, frustrated face and breathed out, low and slow.

'Right.' I tried to echo her usual certainty. 'The birds are a problem. But everything else? We can manage. We can manage.'

Just as she was about to angrily give me a point-by-point rebuttal, there was a knock on the caravan door. The two women from the other night were standing there, Bunty wrapped up with a wide pink bobbled scarf that had seen better days and a tray of something steaming in her mittened hands. The pair made quite the contrast – Sheena's coat was long, patterned with a black-and-white houndstooth, and her gloves, scarf and beret were clearly of the same hot pink set. What linked them was their nature – welcoming and, although they might not appreciate the comparison, grandmotherly.

'Um, hello?'

'Hi, girls. I just wanted to give you something. Welcome you in a neighbourly fashion to the town. Can we . . . come in?' Bunty's voice was muffled by the thick scarf.

There wasn't much space, but we squeezed in and shifted Bruno from the cushioned banquette to the floor. He gave an almighty sigh, but I could tell he had one eye on the warm, sweet-smelling gift in Bunty's hands. Morag is usually in constant motion, and making us four tea worked better at stilling her anxiety than any affection or rationalised statements I could offer.

Bunty removed her scarf, coat and mittens, then pushed the tray towards me. I couldn't be sure, but I thought it was –

'A wee clootie dumpling for you. The clootie was my mother's wedding present from her mother. I never married, you see. Places like Campbeltown have some slim pickings. I mean, I didn't settle here till my fifties – or sixties, was it? Although even Sheena here, who's been here since, oh, I don't know when, she never remarried, did you, hen? Anyhow, but, you understand. My mother's wedding present from her parents was having all her teeth knocked out and replaced by a set of false ones. It was the done thing then. I've always had a sweet tooth, but I'm pleased to say I still have all my own gnashers, and none of this nonsense about brushing twice a day.' She grinned widely as if to show me. Her teeth looked yellow and strong.

I'm always stunned by how quickly a person's life story unravels in front of me. Is it just me? Do others regularly experience the phenomenon of learning more intimate details about a person in the space of a forty-minute train journey than they know about their own mother?

Before we could even take a sip of our tea – thanks to my impatience, Morag knows to add lots of milk to mine so it's cool enough to drink straight away – there's another knock at the door.

It was Donald, from the pub, seemingly in the same fleece from last night. Bunty, Sheena and I naturally cooried closer to give him space to sit, and Morag jumped up to make another cup of tea. Bruno interrogated Donald's legs and crotch thoroughly before jumping and slamming both paws on his knees to get in about the dog-haired fleece. Donald didn't flinch and vigorously rubbed behind and between Bruno's ears – the one ear remaining after some accident in his puppyhood flapped side to side.

'Ahaha, he'll be smelling my one, I reckon. Oh, you're gorgeous, aren't you? Aren't you? Aye, you're a bonny creature all right.' Bruno's tail wagged in assent.

'Sorry the cup's a wee bit cracked. And, uhm, sorry that's the last one we have in here. We're trying to make it by on fewer dishes. Less to wash.'

Donald's eyebrows almost reached his hairline as he inspected the mug's depiction of a morose moggy and the lettering: 'LESBIANS EAT WHAT?' It didn't look like he'd *quite* worked it out, but Bunty certainly had. Morag and I exchanged a look and started to brace.

She said, 'Oh my goodness, girls.' Bunty does that beautiful rhotic r, double-syllabled version of 'girls'.

'Things have certainly moved on from my time. I reckon I could make that into a lovely cross-stitch cushion, what d'ye think?'

And for the next half an hour, we laughed and shared bawdy jokes and tales from our respective youths. I found myself firmly in the moment. It was so bizarre, and beautifully so – us relative strangers, fitting in so well together. Sheena in particular intrigued me – she seemed to be so intelligent, so forthright, so aware of everyone's emotions in the room.

When we first started dreaming of buying this place, of moving here, Morag and I had no clue how we would be treated. It's still rare we hold hands in public, even in the likes of Glasgow or Edinburgh. A situation can flip so suddenly; it just takes one person to disagree with your 'lifestyle' and you're in danger.

Maybe we were wrong to assume homophobia was alive and well in rural Scotland.

We pressed Donald to take some of the remaining clootie dumpling away with him – 'But we only have one other Tupperware, mind, so perhaps you could bring it back soon,' Morag said sternly – and sent all three of them out into the piercingly sunny but still very windy September afternoon, with their promises that they would visit again to help us out. It didn't feel like they were on a gossip-gathering mission like Linksy had been. Although we'd yet to connect with anyone nearer our age, perhaps this was all part of the next stage of our lives, where age didn't matter.

We waved, smiling, through the open door till they left

through the gates. Our smiles disappeared almost instantly. Our fight was merely paused, cordial facades erected for the surprise guests.

'Eilidh—'

'Morag.'

'Don't try your placating voice. We need a plan, we need action, and we need to acknowledge how truly screwed we are.'

I opened my phone for us to look together at our current state of finances, to remind ourselves of our timelines for our various pockets and gaping bags of debt, but there was a Google alert. I'd set it up to send me a notification anytime 'Ardkerran' was mentioned.

'NEW CAMPBELTOWN DISTILLERY ARDKERRAN SET FOR DISASTER' was the headline.

They mentioned me by name several times. The words 'arrogant' and 'naive' burned the screen, as if highlighted in flaming orange. Morag was referred to as simply 'the ex-*Scotsman* journalist' and 'Eilidh's business partner'. They'd be calling us 'just roommates' next. It featured several quotes from disgruntled local residents. The comments section was worse, if anything. The well-written prosaic ones hurt more than the ones blunted by terrible spelling, erratic spacing and capitalisation and excessive use of double and triple exclamation marks.

It was nothing new to me. I've been dished vitriol since I began my blog all those years ago, and then when my book was released. You'd think my skin would be thicker. I thought it was. It had been a long time since I spent hours in bed, tucked up to my chin, screen light blasting my eyes, reading and re-reading all the nasty comments. But they still draw me in, they still hurt.

There is one person in particular – I've never learned their true identity, just know them by their username glencairn_1991 – who comments on my posts without fail. Sometimes it's a simple 'stupid bitch', while at other times it is much, much worse, threats of all horrific kinds. The police did nothing about it when I alerted them, and I refused their suggestions to disable comments. Telling women to disable comments or to mind what they post is almost akin to telling women not to walk home alone at night or not to wear certain clothes. As if it's our behaviour that has to change. Still, those first years of the blog and everything that came with them were pivotal in me becoming who I am now.

It was how I met my editor, Margaret. She worked for a small Scottish press whose aim was to highlight Scottish history and Scottish culture, and she said she was enamoured with my writing style, the way I fused whisky and philosophy and much more besides. She approached me – and she helped me pull together my disparate blog posts into something grander, something with chapters. Margaret forced me to face the handful of negative criticisms – 'Use it to fuel you. Succeed out of spite!' she said in our first phone conversation. It was she who persuaded me to take the negative comments on board, to elevate my writing. Even some of glencairn_1991's were fair – aside from the vehement misogyny and straight-up bile, they − or I am assuming *he* − had pulled out some fair points. Perhaps that's why they hurt even more, because I knew they were right.

All of the quotes in the article Morag and I were reading were anonymous. Some even had good points − about outsiders coming in without knowing the particular needs of the area, about other businesses and people who had come before us, picked up a few grants to build windfarms and the like, promised jobs and then taken the money and run. Not that we intended to run, but who could know how this would pan out? Maybe we couldn't cut it. Maybe, just maybe, the bodies of the men were a terrible omen and we would face terrible repercussions for trying to hide them.

The comments were from multiple different people. They could be from anyone in this town. We don't even know who served us our injunction. Morag finished reading before me and was already standing up again, pacing, onto thinking about next steps, how we might find and even pay for a lawyer. I couldn't follow what she was saying. The sound cut out for a moment and was replaced by a high-pitched ringing in my ears.

The sky turned severe, the heavens opened, the caravan trembled, and for a while it felt like it was just us three, out at sea, in the midst of a storm.

CHAPTER 12

You
1984

The past two years have been a dream. Whisky Ambassador. You don't deal with war and peace, yet you hold that soft power – helping Scotland exert its influence globally via culture, and what's more universal than food and drink? You are the ambassador for not only Ardkerran, but also for Campbeltown, not least for Scotland herself.

And you – you are building yourself.

No matter where you go, Campbeltown is still the centre of the world. That hard-to-reach, gale-sodden peninsula is what everything else connects back to. The mist in your eyes is always real as you regale with tales of Campbeltown Loch, the bewitching Davaar Island, its long shingle path only accessible at low tide, like the house in the horror story 'The Woman in Black', the numbers of keen walkers that pilgrimage along the Kintyre Way, the particular flight patterns of the peregrines. No matter how many times you describe Campbeltown in these foreign places, no matter how tangled the knots of negative feelings attached to the place become, it is ever-present. But you are stronger for leaving it behind.

It was a mutually agreeable arrangement. They wanted you out of their road, to *stop fussing*, and you wanted to escape the familiar suffocation of your beloved town. Absence makes the heart grow fonder, as they say.

Tonight, you are in Japan. On the island of Hokkaido, to be precise. Over forty years ago, Masataka Taketsuru came to Campbeltown to learn the trade from the Whisky Capital of the World, and here stands just one of his resulting creations. He even found his love in Scotland, Rita, and they moved to Japan together. He also spent time in Speyside, but folk from back home generally neglect to mention that.

You have an interpreter, and although you wouldn't consider your accent strong, they are having a bit of a tough time, especially when you talk fast and pepper in your usual amount of Scots words.

'Here is a twelve-year Ardkerran. Note the darker reds, the blush of the liquid, compared to the previous dram. This came from a sherry cask, and draws its colours as well as its flavours from the wood. Dinnae stick yer neb right in – *do not put your nose all the way into the glass*. Let it come to you. What sweet things can you compare it to?'

Hokkaido was chosen for the site of Taketsuru's distillery because of its landscape's similarities to Scotland and the belief that geography is a key component in the character of whisky – and you do believe it is, and therefore you have your doubts about how similar their whisky can be to your country's. Their diverse alpine plants are nothing on heather. From this third-floor conference room, you can just about make out the sea, and if not the sea, then the familiar layering of the blues and greens and greys only ever found wavering above an ocean.

It is a room of men, wearing suits and ties indistinguishable from one another, the only marker of difference in attire being their briefcases, and even then, you note it is a mere divergence in shade of leather or in choice of metal for the clasps and locks. You adore that they are taking notes – it's the sort of thing you do, and the sort of thing you think everyone should do. How do people remember anything otherwise? It shows you're listening, taking it all in, wanting to add to your repository of knowledge rather than allowing this to be an ephemeral moment lost in time. It is a moment to be revisited.

You were invited by Takeshi Taketsuru, the nephew and adopted son of the founder. Whisky has not gained a foothold here yet, but what they are doing is stunning.

In your meeting yesterday, just you and Takeshi (and Söta the interpreter between you), you were both enraptured, eager, ecstatic to have found someone as spirited about the spirit as you.

What makes a whisky Scottish, or Japanese?

Why can't consumers have the experience of the blenders and enjoy cask-strength whisky?

Does terroir even influence the sensory perception post-maturation?

What is the difference between peat from the rivers

of Campbeltown and that of Ishikari River? Should we char our casks? Why would one sell a single malt? How do we elevate our whiskies across the world? Can we persuade film directors to have their characters sampling a fine dram?

This is the most energised you have felt in a very long time. It is almost what you had with them, those men whose names you cannot bear to remember, whose faces appear in your dreams.

The tasting today serves multiple purposes. You are hoping Yoichi Distillery will buy some stock straight from Ardkerran to create a transnational blend. You are hoping to learn from some of the finest craftsmen in the world, who seem to be able to enhance anything they put their mind to. You are hoping to influence the Japanese tongue and hearts towards whisky – and this is Yoichi Distillery's hope too.

The tasting itself doesn't get very exciting, not for you anyway. In your mind, a tasting is only as good as the conversation that flows around it, as good as the setting you're in, the context. Your buzzing brain from days of exploration plus yesterday's conversation with Takeshi helps the context. The setting, while somewhat urban, has views of rushing waters and skies of unfamiliar yet uncannily similar seabirds to those you're used to. But the conversation today is stilted. It feels forced: staccato sentiments blurted out rather than an overlapping of ideas. It's not their fault – this is new to them, and you struggle to convey your usual warmth and wit through an interpreter.

Plus, Söta seems intimidated by you – or maybe confused by your unusual expressions – you're not sure.

Despite that, after the tasting, you and Söta continue your conversations. He walks you back to your hotel. Away from the confines of work, he is more relaxed. He touches your arm several times. You invite him in for a drink. The bar does not serve whisky and your laughs startle the bartender. Sake, then. Söta insists on cold sake – that way you can taste the complexities and quality better. He mimics you from earlier – he loves the word 'neb' too – and you treat the moment like a tasting. A savouring. A sample. Slow and appreciative. Sometimes you approach life this way – you have to, don't you?

You like to imagine the apocalypse happened, the end of days. Ash falling. Fires burning. This moment is your last moment. Whatever you have in front of you to taste is the last one you'll ever have, and you let it linger on your tongue – it works for everything, from oatcakes to chocolate to sex.

This is how Söta is too, with you, upstairs, later, and for the rest of your week-long trip to Hokkaido.

CHAPTER 13

Eilidh
2023

The storm lasted the better part of a week.

Morag, in an uncharacteristic wobble of a moment, had locked herself into the caravan toilet, the only working toilet for a half-mile radius, except the builder's Portaloo, and, well, I felt I'd rather not.

'I didn't think you'd freak out this much. I thought I'd married a stable intelligent third-wave feminist,' I said, hoping a lightly scathing tack would jolt some sense into her.

'Yes, Miss I'm-Young-Enough-To-Allow-TikTok-To-Rot-My-Brain. I just didn't think it'd be like this,' she retorted.

She'd found her first grey hair – on her fortieth birthday – and it was probably not the time to remind her that I'd found my first one four years before and that she regularly stroked my raccoon stripes when we cuddled in front of the telly.

'Morag, babe, it's all groovy, you know? Just let me see. More importantly, *let me pee!*'

The door opened slowly; her head bowed. I couldn't see what she was talking about and I told her so, commanded her to hold the hair out for me to inspect.

Except, she raised her arm much higher than her head. Except, it was a single shining strand in a tuft of brown – a curly grey armpit hair.

I guffawed like a donkey, but managed to wedge my foot into the doorway before she slammed it shut completely on me. I yanked it open, pushed her out and finally relieved myself.

Once the rush turned to a tinkle, I asked her: 'If our roles were reversed, what would you say to me?'

It was like I could hear her lips move into a pout.

'I'd tell you to shut up and stick on some She Drew The Gun.'

We were embracing again before I'd even washed my hands.

'This isn't like you,' I said soothingly. 'You – you've been a hairy take-down-the-patriarchy lesbian since your teens, eschewing beauty standards left and right. What's up? Is it . . . the renovation? The injunction thingy?'

I remembered when I first met her. It was 2012, and she was dating someone else, which only made me obsess over her more. Morag had started writing for *The Scotsman* straight out of uni. Family connections, she said. By the time I met her, she was already the column editor for Food and Drink, and there she was, with her bright yellow frames, kooky earrings and vintage blazer, scribbling in shorthand in a brown leather notebook. I was leading a masterclass event at the whisky festival on Islay, and she made it a point to interview me – I was the only woman represented on the line-up that year, aside from the poet Liz Lochhead. The only one there represented as a whisky expert, anyway.

As she talked and scrawled, her earrings bobbed and shook and I was enamoured. Morag had done her homework – much more than other journalists I'd met, who thought they knew what whisky was but had really only a passing notion of whatever bottles they shared with their dads at Christmas.

No matter how lovely and cool I thought she looked, it was this, her knowledge, her curiosity, which ignited the spark in me. I couldn't tell you now where my confidence came from, but I invited her to spend time with me on the island, and it was during a morning walk along the shore that I oh so casually enquired as to her current dating life. Although she then proceeded to tell me about her partner, my heart skipped with hope at the term 'partner', and soon after leapt at the reference to a 'she'. She.

We kept bumping into each other too, at different events sometimes months apart, and I didn't refrain from emailing her articles I thought 'might be of interest', to keep me in her mind. Finally, after two years of this, she and her girlfriend broke up, which she told me in a bar a couple of streets away from the event we were both supposed to be attending. That drink turned into a few, and that day turned into a few, and before we knew it, we had spent four whole days and nights together. I moved into her flat in Edinburgh within the month. I watched every morning as she selected from her different coloured glasses to suit her mood, suit her attire, how she did this disgusting hacking thing every time she brushed her teeth, how she could soothe me with a look. I always wondered what she noticed of me, what she liked about me, but I never asked. Anyway, it just worked. We weren't counting the days we had spent together, we weren't marking it off, because it felt so right, so normal.

But perhaps I didn't understand the weight of changing our lives so much, moving so far away, taking on such a big endeavour.

As I waited for her to reply to my question about what was up with her, I thought how lucky I was that she'd interviewed me that day and that we'd chosen each other.

Morag didn't speak for a while. She stroked her underarm hair and then my back, and finally rested her head deeply into my neck.

'I . . . I miss my friends. September is zooming by, and I just want a wee pumpkin spiced latte, all right? I want to go for a spontaneous night out. I want to get a massage from that place I like for my birthday. I want a flipping decent pizza.

'And, yes, of course the reno is doing my head in. We've seen enough *Grand Designs* to know it never goes to plan, although at least we know neither of us is going to have a surprise pregnancy, but I never expected all this. But you know what else is doing my head in? You – sneaking around and thinking I don't know what you're doing, thinking you're so clever – researching those . . .' She said the next bit through gritted teeth. 'Dead men.'

She moved away from me. She was right – I had been obsessively googling, looking for answers.

She continued: 'I don't want to think about them – at all. It makes me feel sick now. Really, genuinely sick. Can you please actually help me? What you promised wouldn't happen is already happening. Not even two months in, you've moved on. A new obsession, hyperfixation, whatever you want to call it. I know the signs. You *said* you wouldn't get bored of the distillery – I said again and again – *we are in this for years*. Even if we sell it once we do it up, but no, no–'

'You know it doesn't work like that,' I protested. 'I can't exactly choose what I focus on, what swirls around the forefront of my brain. I certainly don't choose to have "The Grand Old Duke Of York" stuck on a loop in my head several times a week. Anyway, they mostly only last two weeks, and my whisky obsession has remained. I don't know why. But I am here, I am helping–'

'Eilidh, please! *If* we are going to hide these bodies, I need us to really hide them. If this is the decision we have made, I don't want to hear about their existence. I'm starting to feel even more guilty. Gross. Those men . . . who knows who's still grieving them, if they even deserved anything close to what's happened to them. Maybe, since a lot of the building is pretty much on hold, we should do it now, call the police, "rip the Band-Aid off", as the Americans say.'

I was aghast, and I rarely use that word.

'Morag, absolutely not, for all the reasons we already discussed, not least because we don't know how long they could shut us down for – and we don't know if the murderer – or murderers – are still here. It's not safe.'

'Then promise me you'll stop hunting for clues – as you say, it's not safe.'

Stopping my hunt for clues was the last thing I wanted to do. We may not have had a proper toilet, and we might have been getting a bit of cabin fever in this caravan together, no matter how many cute tiny potted plants and fairy lights we hung around the place, but our foresight in getting super-duper satellite internet meant the draw of research was too much for me to resist. Plus, I had barely scratched the surface of the Aladdin's Cave – which, as a room, had started to occupy its own space, inside my brain of many rooms.

'Can we compromise? I won't tell you anything about it. I won't research for more than an hour a day.'

She made a gruff 'hhhmm' noise like Marge Simpson does.

'Fine. I don't want to hear anything about it. I know you think this discussion is over, but it is an open-ended one, okay? Nothing is final. You have to be up for us talking through this again. It's too big.'

'Okay,' I conceded, 'That's more than fair. Now, can I check your nipples for errant greys, you iron goddess?'

She barely pretended to bat away my hand, and her giggle rang clear and true.

We spent the afternoon topless, full of tea, the teapot having grown quite chilled despite the worn Xena the Warrior Princess tea cosy.

Neither of us had realised, but we hadn't been intimate since the night we found the bodies. I suppose that would be enough to turn anyone off it for a while. But in among our afternoon of tender and shuddering orgasms, we hatched a plan.

Morag was to go through to Edinburgh for a week, stay with her parents, leave me to progress the jobs here, pick up my slack. She quickly filled the back of an envelope full of things she was going to do while there. A new piercing, a full-body massage, food at Paradise Palms, drinks with Willow, Blair and Indigo. All the things she'd missed.

Even I'd admit, since the ferries had stopped for the season till March, I was starting to feel a little claustrophobic myself. Morag was going to have to take our battered little Suzuki to get back to what I still kept thinking of as 'the mainland' – even though this peninsula is technically connected to it.

I tried to convince her to get the teeny tiny plane to Glasgow, but it's expensive, and she'd not been dealing well with the intense wind here on the ground as it was, so the thought of being buffeted about up there was not something she would entertain for even a second.

I planned to progress the renovation, of course I did. And she knew, she must have known, that I'd be using this week to get my research of the murders out of my system.

Win–win.

CHAPTER 14

You
1985

You're in Galicia, Spain, when you hear the news. You're in bed with Marie, a full-bodied red, just like the wine she creates, although the area is really more famed for its whites. The folds of her torso are mesmerising to you. Her plump arms squash into her breasts. She radiates warmth.

You've been awake for a while now, managed to slip out of bed and back with a coffee without disturbing her. You remain undressed. You've spent the last hour intermittently watching her and reading your book, *The Wasp Factory* by Iain Banks, which is decidedly less pleasant than Marie, but still as enthralling.

The phone rings next to you, and her heavy blinks with heavy eyelashes make her even more endearing.

'Queres contestar dunha vez?' she says, her anger muffled by the blankets she's just pulled over her head.

The news is not good. The distillery has been bought out by some rich European eccentric artist type who thinks it will be chic to feature a whisky distillery in their portfolio.

Hugh reckons they already own one of the wee islands off the west coast of Scotland, and Ardkerran is another Scottish stamp to add to their collection – probably going for some bloody tweed-making company next.

You have been made redundant till the new owner decides what they're going to do with the place. They're finishing this round of distillation and that's it for the foreseeable, in the short term at least. The kilos of barley still sat in the silos are going to go to waste. Only two folk have been kept on, two blokes you don't know that well, and only as security.

Some of the casks have already been sold off, but Hugh couldn't be more specific than that, nor did you want to press him further, lest you raise suspicions.

Looks like this is your last day in Spain. You didn't realise till you arrived two weeks ago, but Galicia is known for being particularly wet, and you definitely packed incorrectly for the occasion. There's not been an ounce of sun, but you have learned several Galician words that convey the same as dreich, smirr, and goselet. Tebroso, orballo, chover a caldeiradas. Damp grim day, fine mist, heavy rain. You also didn't know how . . . Celtic Galicia is. They have kilts and bagpipes as their national dress and instruments, and their words for rain have made it into the Spanish lexicon, sliding into the dominant language like Scots into English.

It made you very wistful and homesick, actually. Maybe this call was meant to be.

You and Marie make the most of your last night at Casa Brandariz Galicia.

★

You fly from Santiago de Compostela to Edinburgh, take the train from Edinburgh to Glasgow, and ride the bus from Glasgow to Campbeltown. You finish three books in that time, although to be fair two are brief autobiographies, likely ghost-written, thick with fascinating images of the subjects in their youth and beyond, ageing in front of your very eyes.

You set foot on Campbeltown soil for the first time in over three years.

Before you visit your mother, or visit the distillery, you visit the café that overlooks Campbeltown Loch, and just sit and look. The pseudo-palm trees bend at the neck and their lengthy sharp leaves pull brutally to one side. Even from inside the café, you can hear the bells, the creaking and the clanking from the boats grouped together in the harbour. There's one large vessel loaded with hundreds of long damp logs; it's threatening to throw its load overboard. Murky seaweed churns and gathers at the corners of the piers. There is no one outside in the dark afternoon gales.

Did you miss this? Perhaps.

You missed your mother's smell – how did you forget that? Miss Dior eau de parfum, Lambert & Butlers and sweet oat-smelling wool. She holds you, and squeezes you, and scathingly appraises your new hairstyle with no more than a look. Your dad is at the pub and will likely be there till it closes – you'll see him tomorrow. Your mum understands when you leave after just one cup of tea – the distillery's closure is the talk of the town. If anything, she hurries you along to find out more so she can be the centre of attention tomorrow with the insider knowledge she'll weasel from you first thing in the morning.

You wait till you know most of the daytime workers finish their shifts, then make your way to Ardkerran on foot. Your mother never learned to drive and you sold your car when you left. In the twenty or so minutes of howling rain, you devise several likely scenarios and plan conversations for each.

However, plan number one goes supremely smoothly – walk in like you own the place. You head straight for the main dunnage warehouse, where the two dead men are, hopefully, still bent double inside their barrels, undisturbed.

Filigree cobwebs hang from every dark wooden beam. Ivy-esque plants infiltrate between roof and brick. The black dirt floor is strangely damp.

Fewer barrels line either side of the central walkway than you remember. It chokes you to see the last few years stencilled in white on the lids of so many barrels. Everything carries on, doesn't it, even in your absence? Your brief period at the top, in the fray, as the centre, is crystallised. In the past. You don't know you're in the best days while you're living them.

One of *the* barrels is in exactly the same place as before – by the left wall, in between two bourbon hogsheads. Where the other one once was is now a different sherry butt, one with '1984' stencilled on it. *Where is he?*

'Oi, who are you?'

You spin – it's someone you don't know.

'Oh, hi, I'm—'

Before you tell them your name, your eyes adjust to the additional years on their outward appearance. A rounder belly, a droopier face, a balding head. They recognise you too.

'Jings, it's yourself! Didn't recognise you with that barnet. Come on in for a cuppa.' He takes you up to the copper stills, pulls out a fraying chair for you and sticks the kettle on. 'I thought you'd be more tanned — weren't you in Spain when we called you?'

'Ah, aye, I made the same mistake too. The bit of Spain I was in has the same amount of rainfall as here. Mad, aye?'

You try the Scottish sounds in your mouth again, but they don't quite align like they used to.

You catch up, condense years into minutes, with some gaps left out on your part. Your confidence grows and you start wandering about, a simple nonchalant curiosity, merely picking up pens and glancing through the books idly. The answer as to where the other barrel has gone is not here. These are temperatures and times, not whereabouts of stock.

'Aye, we've got to clear out of here by Wednesday. Can you believe it? Nearly sixty people laid off. And rumour has it, this new owner still hasn't paid the farmers on his wee isle, Eigg or Easdale or something was it? Even after six months. What's the likelihood we'll get our pay-out?'

This might be your last chance to scrabble for the lost barrel — if it's even still here — there's only two days till the site is locked up and guarded, and god knows what'll happen to the stock from then on.

Just as you're about to make excuses to ask for a tour, the phone rings. It's your mum.

Your dad is dead – keeled over a half-drunk pint of Guinness.

CHAPTER 15

Eilidh
2023

The morning Morag left for Edinburgh, I sat down to write out my plan for the week. I became caught up in my thoughts, imagining all the information I'd dig up before the seven days were done. I thought I could have this whole plot sorted once and for all before she even finished her first fruity cocktail at the Friday night drinks with her Edinburgh friends in a few days.

Planning is generally my favourite step to any activity, especially if you count research as part of that stage. The actual doing of the plan . . . not so much. I've become more self-aware as the years go on − a lot of the time, I have to remind myself I am a thirty-something lady because I am so quick to judge others for not having figured stuff out, and here I was, still physically unable to put away my own knickers and socks within the week of washing and drying them. By thirty-six, really, I should have known myself better. But, to my credit, I do know that I am oftentimes better at forgoing the planning step and heading straight to the doing step; or, at least, scolding myself into transitioning to the real task at hand after a somewhat brief period of preparation. The notebooks I have that are full of good intentions could fill a library.

Morag had bestowed her master folder containing the holy Gantt chart, among other things, unto me. I've long ago given up on the notion I could organise something so beautiful as that. On the inside cover was a picture of us, halfway up to the Old Man of Storr on our trip to Skye five years ago. My cheeks are red and my hair is escaping in all directions from my bun, Morag has visible sweat on her forehead, and we both have our fleeces and jackets tied painfully tight around our middles. We somehow caught the island in one of its rare dry and very hot periods. The fairy springs were lacklustre that morning and the usual snowmelt evaporated before it could run down the hills. It was so hot we almost never made it to the top – hence the photograph taken here by a very confused German tourist, in case we didn't carry on.

It hadn't rained for five whole days, and the Talisker whisky distillery had had to halve its whisky production. They told us on our tour, the day after this picture was taken, that if the rain didn't come for another two days, they'd have to stop altogether.

Ardkerran Distillery is so named because of the river Kerran Water to the southwest of us; 'Ard' meaning something akin to 'overlooking the river' or 'high up view of the river'. It was once assumed the name was because the distillery drew our water from it, but it is in fact very erroneously named because we can't even see the river from it. It would be romantic, though, if that was where we sourced our spring water from. Some distilleries even sell their cool clean Scottish spring water along with their whiskies. Unfortunately, ours comes from the same place as the rest of the town's water does – up there, from that hill we most often see photographed behind the iconic Campbeltown steeple.

I'd set myself up in the office above the main dunnage warehouse. It was the only place we really had up and running. Morag insisted we prioritise it because it would be the base of operations, the place we would spend the most time when not in our cramped caravan, and although I grumbled at the time at the effort and expense, I was very grateful for this cosy nook filled with our random knick-knacks and artwork. I had a fresh pot of honeyed chai tea, a fake fireplace crackling on my laptop, Bruno sighing on the sagging green sofa in the corner, and a brand-new notebook. What could be finer.

In one column, I wrote the days of the week. In the next, I wrote in some distillery jobs I remember Morag mentioning for me to do, and the third was blank, to be populated once I finished a brain-dump mind-map of clues and potential locations of future clues thus far in 'The Case of the Malt Whisky Murders', as I had come to refer to it in my head.

I looked at the list of jobs Morag had typed and printed out for me (even with little checkboxes for me to tick off) in her folder and grimaced. We needed to start hiring relevant staff, but that would involve lots of phoning of folk. One of my least favourite jobs.

After half an hour spent doodling and dreaming and designing in my notebook, I realised the plan was a bogey. I was procrastinating, and Morag had already made one for me, and she knows how I work better than I do myself. Nothing to do but get right to it on that moody-skied Monday.

Or maybe . . . go to the pub?

I rationalised my trip to the Drookit Dug as reconnaissance. How else was I going to find out which of the locals were in need of a job and willing to put the work in?

However, I spent the afternoon getting royally and thoroughly drunk, generously accepting the large glasses of red wine bought for me by Sheena – much more dressed down that day, and, as it turned out, the owner of the nearby smokehouse – and the pints of Tennent's passed to me from the ex-fisherman Bob/Rob, whose name seemed to keep changing every time he left his corner by the fire for one himself. And I shared a few wee drams in between those with any tourist who happened to drop in for one or two. I regaled each passing visitor with a whisky-related tale in my hammiest Scottish accent, to give them the experience, you know?

I did learn a few useful titbits, to be fair.

Unemployment was at the highest it's ever been, but don't expect anyone to apply for a job either, Sheena advised me. Donald showed me the video of the police officers caught having a threesome, filmed through a window. It was from a while ago, but still at the top of the town's most-talked-about incidents. I was drawn to the hard round belly of the first officer, the way he walked for his bottle of beer, in between rounds presumably, how self-assured and content he seemed.

I attempted a subtle probe into unsolved local murders. The two men must have been presumed missing, at least? Unless the murderer did such a good job of covering it up. I'm not sure which of the group in front of me were even alive in the seventies, when we assumed the men were whacked round the head and forced into whisky barrels, but if they were still talking about 'the police orgy', as it had come to be known, from a few years ago, then surely these two men would be a mystery still worth discussing in the wee toon's long dark winters?

All that arose from my questioning was a yellow suitcase, found bobbing along the water's edge – Sheena was there that day. She and her now ex-husband watched it slowly traverse the side of the pier, through the thick seaweed, to arrive at the esplanade. Her ex was the one to fish it out, nearly pulling himself into the sea with it in the process. People waiting for the bus to Carradale, already twenty minutes late anyway, drifted over to investigate too.

Inside was a dead body – identity still unknown to this day, and presumed to have been tossed into the sea and floated over from Oban.

But my new crew, composed of Donald, Rob and Sheena, quickly moved past it and turned to another common talking point – where all the money goes from the distilleries in town.

A minute number of the population have fancy cars and even fancier houses, but everywhere else in town is sadly likely to be peppered with damp walls, cracked bricks, doors thick with curled-up paint streaks and gardens strewn with weed-choked discarded trolleys.

It's not just where the money goes from the *profit* made on the drink. On Islay, the tax paid on the whisky manufactured there equals £200,000 per island resident. It will be lower here in Campbeltown, but still, when was the last time the government reinvested here? At least, that's what the crowd of three told me in between our great gulps of drink. Even Donald started taking drinks once the sun was fully set, which seemed to happen awfully quickly.

My intention was to simply appear as though I was keeping up with the drinking, warm them up to grease secrets from them and use my intuition to sense their stake in getting to know me.

Except I reached the point where I threw up for the first time in maybe a decade. I think it was switching to Baileys that did it for me – usually the creamy stuff is soothing to my belly, but I'd lost count of the other drinks I'd had, and all of a sudden, I felt as if it was curdling in me.

I was drunk enough to invite them all back to the distillery, to sample straight from the casks, to show them round. It only took one night of Morag being away for me to feel lonely. Usually I'd begin thinking how much I'll appreciate time to myself, how many books I'll manage to read or maybe that I'll finally complete a jigsaw puzzle. Instead, I do foolish things like this just for some company, and in this case, I also thought I'd genius my way through their facades and unlock the mysteries of the murders in one night – or something.

Even as we splashed through the rain, the wind blowing so hard we had to lean dramatically forwards in an attempt to stay upright, I realised what a mistake I had made. I didn't know these people, and I'm certainly not as sly or clever as I think I am, especially when that drunk.

But I didn't want the evening to end, and soon we were guddling among the dust of the Aladdin's Cave, whiskies left to one side in our shared enthusiasm for all these weird wee bits and pieces.

'Here, look at this!'

We rushed to see what Sheena had discovered. A cooper tool of some kind – a large hammer-type thing, wrought-iron, covered in some kind of–

'Blood! Right? This is blood, isn't it?' Sheena said.

'Nah, give it here. Is it not rust or something?' said Donald, scratching the splotches with his wide ridged thumbnail.

The ex-fisherman took it next. He brought the tool right up to his left eye, then pushed his glasses high on his forehead so he could draw it even closer. I saw it bend his pale eyelashes backwards. The three of us shared a look – *he is strange and intense, but let the man work*, we seemed to communicate between us.

And then the crazy bastard licked it!

My stomach roiled again and I spat thick vomit into one of the paint tins. It was crusted with hard paint, still lidded, and I watched as the creamy phlegm slid down the side, casting a wet patch onto the dust.

I felt my cheeks flush with embarrassment before I turned around. What would they think of me?

Except they were too focused on the mallet to notice. All three were now clutching it, raising it high; it was like I was observing some strange religious ritual or pre-battle ceremony, and they were about to swear allegiance to a higher power.

How much do I tell them? Who knows who they know? Who knows how easily anything I say to them could spread out in this community?

But I was bursting to let them in on it all – they were all so excited, and maybe it was the drink and the fiercely intense afternoon spent with these lovely people, or the feeling I'd had here, the feeling that the rest of the world doesn't exist, that it's just us on this headland, but I felt a quick and keen kinship spring up between us.

What would Morag think? She'd been gone less than a handful of hours, and already I'd drawn attention to myself and our grisly secret. Not that the mallet definitely was *the* murder weapon, but . . .

'I wonder if . . . d'ye think we could get someone to, like, test it or that? Scan for DNA.'

'Nah, nah, it's old, it's bone-dry. Well, though, maybe. Does that matter?'

'It's . . . beautiful, don't you think?'

It was Sheena who said that last part, a kind of golden awe in her voice. My connection to her felt even stronger again. It was fascinating. It was beautiful. In a dark sort of way.

I stepped closer to the group, and they parted, almost ceremoniously passing the object to me.

I examined it fully, turning it over in my hands, rubbing its roughness through my palms and tracing the outlines of drops and drips and rivulets of blood. It was hard to see against the black of the metal and in between the orange of the rust, but it was there all right.

As if someone had used it to smash a skull. Or even two.

'I can tell ye, that's an old shipbuilding tool. I can't mind the name, but it's a mallet for opening seams.' Rob bothered the tufts of white hair that stuck out in a ring around his head – was he trying to make the thoughts come more easily or was he nervous about something? He looked almost as pink as me, though not as wobbly. The capillaries around his bulbous nose seemed to glow a darker purple than before.

'So what's it doing here?' Sheena asked.

I had an answer: 'Most cooper's tools were repurposed from elsewhere. Old farming equipment usually, but I bet round here there were plenty of shipbuilding tools to purloin.'

Donald was the first to ask the most pertinent question. 'But why is there blood on it?'

I aimed to keep them talking by asking more questions.

102

'Well, another way to ask Sheena's question then is, why is this, with blood stains on it, here? Why not cleaned or hidden away?'

'Well, I did find it in the hidden hidey-hole.'

'The *what*?' the rest of us exclaimed simultaneously.

Sheena took us over to the corner she'd been rustling around in and, lo and behold, there was a hole. A large brick-shaped hole.

'I noticed the paint around the bricks here looked much fresher than the rest, so I took a screwdriver and scraped it between the bricks, and it went right through the edge of this one.'

I saw the screwdriver, covered in white paint dust, and the piles of flecks in a line along the floor. I looked at the bricks around it, moving my eyes in a wider and wider spiral, spreading out from the open hole at its centre.

Sheena's hands were shaking. Ever so slightly, but I could see her try to hide the tremor.

'What else is in there?'

'Oh, nothing really. Um, just that hammer. Nothing else. I haven't had a proper look though.'

I'm not sure I believed her, then. Would it be rude to ask her to empty out her pockets before she left?

I knelt on the floor and wondered if I dared to put my hand in.

I brushed my fingertips against the base of the cavity, disturbing more dried paint flakes, then stopped. I leaned down, got to eye level and pushed the heel of my hand into the brick. Darkness. Then I pushed my other hand in as far as my wrist. Nothing. I pressed my shoulders against the wall, and my arm went all the way in. I still couldn't feel the back; there was nothing but cloying air. I patted the floor of the cavity. Something rustled. I yanked my arm out.

The others were watching, wide-eyed.

I tentatively put my arm in again, imagined in my mind's eye the space I had felt. A whisper emanated from where my hand met the hard base, but I persevered.

There was something there, but it was too hard to grasp from that angle. I twisted my whole body and just managed to grip something between my fingertips.

I drew it out.

It was paper – half damp, half crisp.

Letters, love letters. I could tell from the words I could read at a glance. I spread them out on the nearest table.

Without speaking, we divided the sheets between us to examine as a team. None were complete, all were partially mice-nibbled or wavy from water, but there were places where the ink remained true. I've always found heavy cursive handwriting difficult to decipher, but between us we pieced together one side of a relationship – a relationship that seemed to have been hidden. Until now.

It had all the hallmarks of a secret homosexual relationship – it's the kind of language I'd seen used before in archived diaries and letters I'd read over the years in my deep dives into queer history – but they also used some kind of codewords or pet names, so I couldn't be certain that they were two people of the same gender.

We turned as one to Donald's gasping laughter. 'These

are . . . well, I think I've learned a thing or two about how to woo. This is beautiful. Although I might get a slap as likely as a kiss for a couple of these.'

Sheena was blushing – I probably was too. Rob was rubbing his hair again and contemplating every relationship of his long life compared with the one we had sneaked a glimpse into.

I used the pause as an opportunity to chivvy them out of the building, by pulling them together towards the door and offering a toast.

'To this unknown couple, may we have such a connection as they did. Slàinte Mhath!'

They all wanted to come back again, they'd all caught the bug of intrigue. And who could blame them?

As long as Morag didn't find out, this was fine, right?

CHAPTER 16

You

1985

The new owner still hasn't visited, although it's been at least six months since he purchased the distillery. No one new has been hired, no one has been rehired, no one has received their final pay, and no one, not even the most expert diggers and needlers for gossip in this town, know what the hell is going to happen next.

And you can't get in to do anything about the barrels. With the dead bodies. Of the men you killed over a decade ago. The men who now, with time and space and reflection, did not deserve such deaths. Did they? Maybe. Now you have grieved for your father, you see the ending of life more clearly.

You have spent time with your thoughts, your memories, your guilt. Most of the moment of murder is blocked out, possibly for ever. You remember the feeling, though – the feeling they gave you. That's the only thing that still gives you pause, the only thing that nags at you that maybe you were right to do it.

And it still wasn't enough to save this town. Or your beloved distillery. Or you.

You still walk past that way most days. There's a hole aching in your heart for what you have lost. Even all these years away, all the time spent being able to look at Campbeltown from the distance of hundreds or thousands of miles, you thought the distillery was a constant. That sweet smell of fermenting yeast is gone.

Maybe you're hallucinating, but you keep smelling blood in its stead. A sharp, tangy stannic spurting scent that cuts through everything else.

And maybe you're probably definitely hallucinating, but you keep seeing them.

Them.

Sometimes it's just at first glance, someone walking towards you on the street looks like one of them. Sometimes it's two wavering apparitions, waving at you from the other end of the bar, raising a glass when you raise yours. A nod. Sometimes you nod back.

Sometimes Duncan is pouring tea from the teapot, the one you bought as a gift for him, knowing he wanted one but was too unsure of how he'd be perceived if people knew he coveted such a thing. He pours and he pours and he pours and the cup never fills. Sometimes it's not tea. Sometimes it's whisky – it looks the same, but you can smell it's different.

Sometimes it's blood.

CHAPTER 17

Eilidh

2023

Over the week that Morag was gone, I tried everything to keep my mind busy, my hands busy, to not keep looking for clues. I knew I would only get myself in trouble. Once I had sobered up from the other night and was full of sweet milky tea and kiwi-flavoured vape, I gave myself a stern talking to. I rehearsed what I would say to each person, individually or as a group, if Donald, Rob or Sheena asked to come up and investigate again.

I picked up an old cross-stitch I'd designed a while back, a quote from a favourite TV show surrounded by oranges and lighthouses and curling tentacles, but even with a ghost story podcast filling the background and my mind, it felt slow and clunky in my hands. I had begun a 2,000-piece puzzle, then remembered how long they took once I was a few hours in and had barely finished the bloody border, and subsequently started and abandoned a 1,000-piece puzzle. I'd neglected my blog for weeks by that point, but it didn't seem appealing either. To be fair, it was an almost unbelievable feat that I had managed to post so religiously for so many years before that point.

My final post, published online in August, the morning we set off in our caravan followed by our removal van to make the long slow journey towards our new home, had explained how I would be taking a sabbatical, my first in fifteen years, and the comments underneath were mostly warm and grateful for my dedication so far, wishing me a good time building my new distillery, excited for my first updates. I felt I couldn't post again – not knowing what I knew now about the truth behind this distillery. At least two men were murdered here, but I had never come across the story of their disappearance in my extensive searches into Ardkerran – I'd even found a black-and-white video on YouTube filmed here in the early seventies and narrated with a clipped RP accent – but there was zero mention of anyone going missing.

Had it just been hidden or did no one care that they were gone?

I really did try to do everything except think about these men, and I even managed to get some jobs done in my attempts to push my thoughts of them away – we now had several new(ish) mash tuns coming from a Speyside distillery that had recently upgraded theirs, and I had finally tracked down the one man in the country who could service our hundred-year-old grain mill.

But the men were ever present at the back of my mind. Or the side of my mind. I see and hear multiple things at once sometimes, as if I have many threads to follow or several screens alight in front of me. I used to find it annoying, and when I remember to take my ADHD meds it usually narrows down to one image, one sound, but now I love how I can offer so many thoughts and ideas at once. Not everyone can.

I started getting into the habit of going to the Aladdin's Cave after my dinner – usually a Chicken and Mushroom Pot Noodle without the soy sauce in it because I'd sook most of it straight from the sachet while I waited for the kettle to boil. I kept telling myself it was just for a place to read or work, but really it was to surround myself with all of these things, to let my imagination run, to have space to think outside of the tiny caravan and the too-tidy office.

I held out till the Thursday night, when I decided I deserved to sit and read through the documents we had found with the photographs. Some were letters from bottlers, one side of a negotiation for prices and stock. There were several cloth-covered books, frayed and chewed, filled with hand-written columns of numbers, of barley weights, of heights of barley-steeped liquid over time, of malt-turnings, of kiln temperatures, of peat stock. There weren't columns for the years, but I managed to work out from the dates and days which years they were referring to. The handwriting in the distilling-room ledgers changed in 1971. It was a small change, but the tail on the number nines went from straight to curved and the sevens had the addition of the little line across to make clearer that it is a 7, not a 1, like my mother taught me to do – she used to do accountancy, and it stuck.

I compared the writing to that of the letters Sheena found and I thought they could be a match – the writing from before 1971, not after.

There were a few possible names for the murdered men that came up in the distiller's weekly summary to the owner – Roger, Duncan, Alistair, William, Hugh and James. The letter-writer had to be one of them. Maybe the recipient was also one of them. I couldn't be sure of any other men's names from that time period. The head distiller remained the same until the distillery closed in 1985, so he couldn't be one of the casked cadavers. Could he be the murderer, though? The photograph, my main clue, was definitely taken before 1971 – the men seemed younger in it. But then, it's not like I could google what being preserved in whisky for decades could do to someone's face.

Knowing no builders or anyone else could question my sanity, I spent Sunday morning tracing and tapping all of the bricks across the distillery, in case of another hidey-hole.

That was where I found the shirt. A small nook in a side room to the main distilling room that I wouldn't have known was there except I was tracing my fingers along the walls as if I were lost inside a maze. I couldn't be sure it was a man's – it had women's sizing and was buttoned the wrong way for men. But perhaps it was that I couldn't convince myself it wasn't a man who killed them.

I replaced the brick, after checking all others in the vicinity thoroughly, and brought the garment up to the Aladdin's Cave. I stared at it for a long time. The blood stains. The frills of the sleeves were elaborate and enthralling in the way the blood had dripped and seeped along them. It was a blouse like Morag would wear on her most Victorian/pirate-esque days in her twenties. The splotches of brown down the front were too thin to be blood though. I hesitated before sniffing one patch deeply, then I licked it, remembering Rob's confidence with the bloody mallet. Whisky – no doubt about it. Was I looking for a woman, or a flamboyantly dressed man? I placed it in the hole in the wall of the Aladdin's Cave, which was where I had decided to store any clues I found on my way. Away from where Morag would find them.

Finally, on the Monday morning that Morag was due to return, I couldn't help myself.

I *had* to take one more look inside those barrels before she came back. I didn't know when I'd get the chance again, and it had begun to physically hurt me, not knowing if there were key clues hidden inside.

I had been dreaming about them all week. No matter how hard I pushed them away during the day, they visited at night. Dreams that seemed as if I had actually risen straight from my bed, walked to the warehouse and opened the barrels to reveal a trove of secrets. Or sometimes just blood. Sometimes the men were alive, awake, cracking their joints back into place and turning their heads to speak to me. One trying to get his broken watch to work, shaking drops of whisky everywhere.

But when I woke up, in my bed, that Monday morning, it was just me and Bruno and the quilt that had somehow turned a hundred and eighty degrees during the night. Bruno opened one eye at me from the floor, and that's how I knew I'd been tossing and turning in my sleep. He'll usually stand most things for a chance of bed and quilt, but not if he's repeatedly caught in the crossfire of my flailing limbs.

I pulled back the curtain of the rain-spattered plastic window of the caravan and watched the clouds move briskly across the pink-tinged sky above the heather-covered hills. Knowing Morag, she would have set off at the crack of dawn, 'just in case'. I had, at most, an hour or two.

Since we had done the business of opening and closing the barrels together once, I convinced myself I could handle it alone, and more quickly than before.

I took a torch, Bruno's dog bed and some pocket meat – Peperamis – for the job ahead. As soon as we stepped outside, he started trying to shake the falling raindrops from his fur and get back inside.

'No, no, puppy, do your business and then we've got work to do.'

Smacking the first metal hoop off and over the top of the barrel was easy enough – satisfying even – I pretended I was a fearsome warrior or a burly blacksmith. I then bashed the lid of the barrel in the exact spot the man in the YouTube video had advised, and it flipped up just right. A moment later I realised I should have worn gloves, but I didn't feel the scratches and grazes somehow and my grip was just strong enough to yank it off.

I peered in. The man's trousers had pulled down,

and I was presented with a classic case of builder's bum, white and glistening through the green-hued liquid, a few stray hairs drifting in between the cheeks like a strange sea anemone.

I'd decided this time the easiest thing to do was to pull them out from the liquid, without decanting.

I mean, I managed it, but not without spilling disgusting whisky all down my front and my arms getting soaked to the shoulders, but he was there, on the floor again.

Except . . . he was missing a hand.

I recoiled and gagged at the open wrist, the flesh's ragged cross-section laid bare.

What. The. Actual. Fuck.

I looked inside again. Should I plunge my arm in and feel about, like some macabre dive for treats in a bucket? Did we somehow miss this the first time we came across the bodies? Surely not. But if it's not there . . .

I flashed the torch beam. I could see it, at the bottom. It had a large ring on the pinkie finger.

Just in case, I took a quick look around me. I felt like someone or something was watching me, but there was only Bruno, sleeping soundly, somehow with his back paws stretched up near his chin.

Using two measuring sticks, one in each hand, I attempted to squeeze them down either side of the dismembered hand and pull it up. It dropped from my makeshift tongs several times, and my frustration rose with each ghastly plop that caused fat drops of malodorous liquid to jump up towards my face.

Eventually, it was out, and I laid it on the floor behind me. I inspected the body first.

I noted the brand of his fancy calendar watch, wrote down the exact date and time it stopped, and barely paused before I decided to take a video on my phone. I turned the body over and around, filming every angle.

The bruising on his left elbow, the hole in his head above his right ear, the label inside the tongue of his leather brogues. I considered narrating, like a pathologist from *NCIS*, but something moving in my peripheral vision stopped me.

A shuffling noise emanated from the doorway and I whipped round – but there was nothing there.

I swung the phone back to the body and continued, breathing heavily.

When I turned around to capture the hand, it was gone.

My heart stopped.

I rose to full height and assumed a defensive stance, phone still filming.

Bruno stretched luxuriously, then jumped up and started sniffing deeply.

But he didn't come towards the pungent barrel and body – he snuffled towards a row of barrels.

I tentatively stepped that way too, then Bruno's bark made me jump and drop my phone.

Out from behind the barrels came the filthiest scruffiest little dog I had ever seen. And it had the hand in its jaws. It growled with its canines exposed, and a chase ensued, me chasing Bruno, chasing the dog.

We ran, like some ludicrous Benny Hill skit, this way and that way, in and out of the rows of barrels and wooden pillars. The scruffy dog eventually worked its way into a gap that Bruno couldn't squeeze through and the growls intensified. Bruno retaliated with a high-pitched persistent bark usually reserved for squirrels who have eluded him by running up a tree.

'Shh, shut up, Bruno, please, shh!'

Bruno gave one final woof! and sat neatly on his haunches, waiting for me to assist him in the hunt.

I thought for a moment. Then I rootled around in my dungaree pockets – somewhere, in among the old tissues and dog poo bags and half-empty pill packets, I knew there were treats lurking. I excavated them from the mess of rubbish in my palm and held them towards the nook in which the small scruffy dog was vibrating. I attempted a soothing voice, placating it to come towards me, assuring it that I was a safe person.

There was a light thud as, I assumed, the hand fell to the floor and the dog leapt out to lick and nibble the treats in my hands. Bruno pawed me heavily to remind me he had been a good boy and those should be his treats.

I awkwardly pulled a few more out of my right pocket with my left hand, keeping my other arm outstretched towards the scruffy wee dog.

I've got myself into some strange scrapes before, and my pals do seem to enjoy my rambling 'Eilidh's random adventure' voice notes, but this one took the biscuit. And I had no one to share it with.

I was left with both dogs sitting patiently, tails sweeping like windscreen wipers across the dusty floor. What now?

The new dog did not have a collar. I knew some islanders and farmers might let their dogs roam free, but I wasn't sure whether that was normal in a place like this. It tilted its head at me and I gave it a scratch behind the ears. I took a quick look at its downstairs and saw it was a male, balls and all.

His leg started thumping the ground – I'd clearly found a favoured scratching spot. Bruno whined for attention too, and soon all three of us were coorie in for scratches and cuddles. It was only then that I remembered I was fusty-blood-whisky-stained and pulled my hands back, but they demanded more.

To be fair, this new dog was so filthy I didn't think I could make a difference. His fur was matted, and dust was pluming off his back as I patted him, leaving my hand somehow dry and sticky at the same time. I guddled for more treats and unearthed the Peperamis, and a plan formed.

I broke them up into pieces and laid a long trail towards Bruno's dog bed. I placed my weather-beaten fleece down as a rug next to it. But the wee dog jumped right into the dog bed, and Bruno just deferred to him and turned and turned and turned till he settled. They seemed happy enough for the moment.

The hand was quite worse for wear – with teeth marks and things straggling out from the bottom of the palm. The skin had pulled off the thumb – *degloved* is the word that surfaced from the recesses of my mind. The signet ring would not budge. The fingers were bloated from the years in liquid.

I laced my fingers into these fingers. Soft and almost gooey. Almost pleasant. Could I snap the pinkie? Was it too spongey?

A few hacks with the sharp end of a hammer managed to separate the finger from the hand, and I marvelled at it. This was gross, no doubt, but also, hopefully, a once-in-a-lifetime experience.

I pulled the signet ring off the bottom of the finger and placed it inside one of my many used tissues, and then I took one final look over the body.

Whatever was in his pockets had turned to mush – but from what I could see it was once paper, with perhaps some traces of blue ink. The labels didn't offer much else except that the suit was made by a tailor called Henson's. I peeled back his left eyelid, and then the right. Bloodshot. Green-yellow irises.

Then I spotted it, clinging to his shoulder.

A long wavy red hair.

Much too long to be his.

Much too long to be any man's, really. Although perhaps I was assuming too much. Didn't lots of men have long hair in the seventies?

I found another tissue to curl the hair up into, then placed both of my finds into a nearby an empty Pot Noodle cup.

118

Just as I was reaching for his watch, the dogs simultaneously started a cacophony of barking.

In the doorway stood my wife.

She looked mad as hell.

CHAPTER 18

You
1995

You left Campbeltown nearly a decade ago, when the ghosts became too much.

You've found your place in Northern Ireland, a distillery on the coast that faces Scotland. You've learned to spell it 'whiskey' and to distil three times and to bite your tongue when a story is told about the superiority of Irish whiskey to Scottish whisky.

You've changed your name too. To be fair, you'd always had an Irish surname – sort of. Your not-too-distant ancestors fled the famine to across the water and they changed their name from Murphy to Murray in an attempt to assimilate, in a place that still proclaimed 'No Irish, No Blacks, No Dogs' in the windows of their establishments, and so you grew up as a Murray. But the Catholic guilt remained through the generations, even once your father married a Protestant lass, and even after you and your brothers renounced religion entirely in your teenage years. The guilt didn't stick enough for you to refrain from murder, you suppose.

So now you are a Murphy, and happy for it. You wonder what your great-great-grandad would think.

Sometimes you call your mum. She doesn't know you've changed your name – she probably wouldn't understand why. You make excuses as to why you can't come to visit.

Sometimes you sit on the beach and imagine you can see the edges of the Kintyre peninsula. Sometimes a familiar bird swoops above your head and you believe it has brought you a message from over there.

Sometimes the ghosts visit here too – usually once you've gone long stretches without remembering them, and usually it's simply a glimpse or a thin apparition, something you can see through.

You can't ever go back home. They will be real and bodied and corporeal there.

CHAPTER 19

Eilidh
2023

Morag didn't say anything, which was worse than if she had started screaming at me. She strode past me and responded instead to the two dogs jumping up at her. She knelt down and spoke calmly to them, querying the new dog and telling Bruno how much she'd missed him. She looked tanned and her freckles were sharp on her cheeks.

'Been to the sunbeds, have you?' I tried.

She ignored that. 'Who's the dog? Don't tell me you've adopted a stray on a whim while I've been gone? A disgusting wee thing who needs a good bath at that. We're in that caravan for at least another three months, Eilidh. We can't fit him in too.'

'But he's only little!' Using my baby voice as an attempt to be cute was the wrong choice in that moment. Morag's expression didn't change. She was far from amused.

I thought about how we got Bruno. We moved swiftly in our early days, and Bruno came to us not long after I'd moved into her kitsch Edinburgh flat.

We were walking home from a night of board games and drinks at a place that only served chicken wings as food. Our bellies were sloshing with alcoholic Oreo milkshakes and our fingers were sticky with all flavours of sauces that neither napkin nor soap could budge. It was dark enough that we felt safe holding hands in the city. Our fingers melded together, both through intense affection and honey BBQ glaze, and we stopped to kiss under a streetlight at the edge of the Meadows.

That's when Bruno came bounding towards us, a black thing out of the black night. We moved away from the road to inspect him more closely and he very obediently followed us, trotting with his tongue lolling out. One ear was raggedy and bleeding, and he had gashes on his muzzle and belly. No collar. I don't remember if we even discussed it – we took him straight home with us.

The following day, the vet couldn't find a microchip either, and we were already smitten. Perhaps we were wrong, but we didn't do much searching for his previous owners after that.

I looked at him in the warehouse, picking out the grey streaks in his eyebrows and muzzle and down his legs. He was still almost as energetic as he was when he first leapt on us all those years ago.

'I don't know who he is – he just appeared about half an hour ago. So, no, I haven't claimed him yet, but he seems to have chosen to stay here, for a while at least. We can ring around, maybe call the police or something, see if we can find his actual owners. He looks like he's been out and about for a while though, wouldn't you say?' I said, trying to tempt her in with a question.

'Hmm. Right. But never mind the dog. This – this here – is the exact opposite of what we agreed before I left. It's stupid, so fucking stupid, opening them up again, especially with random people coming around to inspect the place. Please tell me it's just the one.'

'Yes, I . . . well, I hadn't got to the other body yet, if I'm being honest.'

I noticed she was keeping her eyes above waist height, unless looking directly at the dogs. She was avoiding the body. He was, thankfully, facing away from us.

She was waiting for an explanation. I continued. 'It was burning me up, knowing there was more evidence here, knowing I didn't catalogue anything properly the first time, knowing I could, maybe, probably, solve this in one quick task.'

'And did you?'

'No.'

'Yep, no surprise there. I'm going to unpack and you can sort this out. Things will be opening up soon – the bloody builders are here at twelve, remember, you eejit? So you can spend the morning searching for that wee pup's owner. Thank you and please.'

There was nothing I could say to stop her leaving, to have a fuller conversation, to ask how her week away had been. So I didn't.

I packed away the body and squashed it down a little further than before. I'd managed to lose a few litres of liquid in the process of the morning, so I topped it up with water from the outside tap, sloshing a bucket of it in and ending up with half of it in my shoes.

It didn't take long to find the owner of the dog, though. I called Donald first, thinking he might know as the owner of the local dog-friendly pub and as someone who knows a lot about everyone's business.

'Oh aye, that's Kero. He goes about where he likes. Usually found down on the beach but he comes in here and other places begging a lot. I wouldn't worry too much, just let him go.'

'Okay, well, he's not for leaving.'

'Ah, and d'ye want him to leave?'

'I at least want to know where he's meant to live, whose dog it is, in case anything happens. Plus, he's stinking.'

'Aye, right enough. Give me two ticks and I'll get William's number for you. By the way, had an exciting time the other night. Such fun. Any further in the case, Mademoiselle Poirot?'

I cringed – I'd forgotten I'd asked them to call me that at one point. I twisted towards the door to check Morag wasn't listening in.

'I have found a signet ring . . . um, in another . . . cavity.'

Not exactly a lie, but it was definitely too risky to share the fact that I had more than just a bloody mallet and some letters, that, in fact, I had two pale and lightly bloated bodies and a bloody frilly shirt too.

Donald seemed intrigued. My rehearsed speech for deterring him dried in my mouth.

'Oh, aye. I'll be opening up soon – why don't you come down? Bring the dogs and the ring. I'm in it now, need the next chapter, my detective fix.'

I went to the caravan, with the dogs trotting loyally alongside me. Morag wouldn't answer me properly when I went in. I passed her the folder and a hastily scrawled list of the jobs I did while she was away.

She was placing her clothes into a large blue Ikea bag to take to the laundrette – another concession necessary thanks to us living in a caravan.

'Why don't I take that up the road for you? Anything else I can do while I'm in town?'

She grunted at me. 'Sure. Fill up the car, she's nearly out. Bring back some sandwich things. Olives. I fancy olives.'

Normally I would have strapped Bruno in, clipped the little seatbelt attachment to his harness, but I wasn't sure how to handle both him and Kero. Kero didn't have a collar and he seemed a little free-spirited. Would he even get in a car?

Kero sat at the passenger door, expectantly. I opened it, and he hopped in and settled into the footwell.

'Okay, it's only a five-minute drive, I suppose,' I said to him.

Kero seemed very happy to see Donald when we eventually arrived, especially when Donald broke one large bone-shaped dog biscuit in half to give to them both. Bruno scarfed his in less than a minute and stared down Kero while he finished his.

Before I could even get the ring out of my pocket, someone came in the door and Kero rushed to meet him.

'Oh, hi, William. I don't know if you've met Eilidh yet? She's one of they – one of those women who's doing up the old Ardkerran distillery.'

William nodded in my direction and ruffled Kero's head, then took a seat at the bar next to me. I held out my hand for a handshake. He laughed darkly as he took it.

'Very fancy, eh? Don't think I've shook someone's hand in years.'

'Um, so . . .' I attempted to open up a conversation. 'Does Kero mean something? It sounds vaguely Scottish, is it Gaelic?'

They both laughed at me. 'No, it's short for Kerosene. His sister is Diesel.'

'Let's see that ring then,' Donald said.

I froze.

William looked at me expectantly, then Kerosene jumped up onto his lap. 'Ugh, you are one mucky pup. Remind me to lob you in the loch later, eh? Eh? And what's this about a ring?'

'Oh, the girls have quite the mystery on their hands!' Donald clapped his hands onto the bar 'Sheena found a bloody mallet hidden inside a wall! Letters too. And now Eilidh's found a ring – you brought it, aye? Oh my gosh, and there was someone's ashes too! Nothing written on the urn either! Morag's just back from her week away in Edinburgh too, right? You'll have to update her on everything we found.'

I gritted my teeth. Had I not said to say nothing? I couldn't remember. Did I expect this to stay secret anyway, in a place like this? And how did he know about the movements of my wife?

'Oh aye, let's have a look then.'

I brought the ring out and placed it on the bar. It shone brightly against the worn dark wood.

William immediately picked it up. 'Aye, seen a few folk with those. I want to say it's something to do with the Freemasons or something like that anyway.' I peered closer, but Donald picked it up and took it away before I could take a good look at what he had gleaned from the ring. Donald gave the ring back to me, closed in his fist, and all of a sudden didn't seem as interested in the object. I didn't want to press him, and he steered the conversation away. I tried to work out the look on his face and stored it away to analyse later.

'While you're here, I wanted to run the idea for the next tasting by ye.'

That was the last thing on my mind, but I humoured Donald as he started talking about cocktails and garnishes and infusing drinks with smoke. I was so internally distraught I almost didn't register how incongruous this was with my current view of him as a slightly scruffy man's-man type who would begrudge more than a single ice cube in a whisky. I realised once again that I had let my presuppositions get the better of me.

'Uh, smoke?' I said.

'Aye, I saw it on YouTube. If you've got some spare

staves from barrels, we can roast them with a mini blowtorch thing, place glasses on the top, let the smoke fill them. It's pretty cool, like.'

I had seen it before, and indeed we had thought about how to add some wow factor to our whisky – once we'd made it. Make something social media worthy, in an age where making a damn good product just wasn't enough anymore. I'd rejected it before, when Morag showed me a video she'd saved. I didn't want to be a gimmick and I felt the smoke leaned too much into the masculine . . . but what exactly had we intended when we proclaimed we would 'disrupt the male-dominated world of whisky' when we wrote our crowdfunding copy?

I promised Donald I would bring some old barrel staves next time I visited, and then I took Bruno for a walk around the town.

We'd been in Campbeltown for over a month already, and I had only visited the Tesco so far. I certainly didn't expect a busy town looking like any other in Scotland – a long main street with rows of cafés and gift shops and hairdressers. The Campbeltown Picture House cinema, one of the oldest remaining of its kind, was showing a mix of old and recent releases, and the kebab shops could have been the ones on Sauchiehall Street in Glasgow, plonked here from the sky.

It was the loch that made it all the more unreal, although it reminded me of Oban. Before we moved here, I irritated Morag with my repeated renditions of 'Campbeltown Loch', as I had watched Andy Stewart sing it over and over again on YouTube. J. & A. Mitchell & Co. had even released a blend of whisky with the same name. You can tell they have blended for taste over colour, since no batch is the same shade of amber, and as far as blends go, it does a good job of representing the area – or at least that's what I thought when I first tried it.

· I had romanticised this place, this peninsula, this town cut off from the rest of the country. Now I could see it was like any other in Scotland: beautiful hilly landscapes in the distance and decrepit bookies in the centre.

Maybe it was my mood tempering my view. Morag and I didn't usually fight. It was the first thing we always said, when people asked us the secret to a long and happy relationship – to our long and happy relationship. We talked, we compromised, we paused and thought and came back to each other once we had sorted out our own emotions and why this particular thing had upset us so, what from our respective pasts had influenced the present, before we resumed a disagreement. Usually, we both apologised.

I resolved to go back, once I had completed my errands, and to apologise together.

Except, when I got back, she didn't apologise.

I did. I said: 'I am so sorry; I understand why you're annoyed. I can't help myself sometimes and I think we view this differently. I thought we both wanted to know more about the bodies, about the history of our new home.'

Morag sprang up from the bed and threw her book on the floor. Her yellow glasses tilted off her nose with the force, one leg dangling in the air.

'*I can't help myself.* Do you know how many fucking times I've heard that, Eilidh? I think I thought it was adorable once – your impulsivity, your curiosity, your weird obsessions with macabre stories. Except this is real life. We're not swanning about Edinburgh anymore, with your wee whisky tastings and you writing when you feel like it because I support us with my actual job, which I quit, for this!'

'*You* support us? I think actually it's your parents who do that. I'm sorry I didn't have parents who could *buy* me a flat to live in—'

'I knew it, I knew it. I bloody well knew it. All this time, that's what you've really been thinking, isn't it?' She finished her question with an exasperated sigh. 'You certainly weren't complaining when your second book deal fell through – because you never finished the bloody book, by the way – not because of any one of the other myriad reasons you came up with to excuse yourself to everyone else – and when you moved in with me when we'd barely started dating.'

Bruno moved and sat in between us, stiff, and he whined.

Morag straightened her glasses and placed her hands on her hips, arms rigid. I watched her hands squeeze and unsqueeze her waist. She was trying to be stern, but the movement of her hands revealed her anxiety. We'd not done this before, said these things before, and maybe we should have.

'All I wanted was for us to start afresh here. After being

cooped up in the flat – yes, the one my parents generously paid for, the one you happily called your own and you happily played house in, minus the cooking and cleaning duties that a kept wife stereotypically does–'

'Since when were we stereotypical?' I interjected.

'Since when was a relationship, a partnership, supposed to be so one-sided? I used to think we were a power couple – remember when we used to joke about that? But that's just when things are going well, when things are working. We came here as a partnership – to do something big and great and monumental together, to spend the second half of our lives in a beautiful place doing something most people would only dream of. We had a dream – but the reality is, you can't put the graft in. Well, we're stuck here for now. All I asked was that you do your bit – and as soon as I'm gone, you're doing the worst thing you could do. Reopening those barrels is the most insane thing you have ever done, and I can't . . . I can't deal with this.'

She paused and, without looking at me, said, 'Let's just get through the first few months . . . and then we'll see what we'll do next. About this distillery. About us.'

Morag doesn't cry, but I thought I could see tears forming in her eyes.

CHAPTER 20

Eilidh
2023

Morag wasn't sleeping in the caravan. Bruno was so confused. He couldn't work out who he was allowed to follow round or why we weren't cuddling anymore, all three of us together. We'd been taking it in turns at night, alternating him snuggling with me in the caravan, and with Morag with his dog bed up in the office. Everything felt wrong.

Yet we were stuck. We had to carry on. It was my fault we'd taken on this project and its huge, huge debt. I saw it as the culmination of my career, my way of changing the industry for the better, proving how it could be done. But it tasted ashen. At once a boring and impossible challenge and tainted with whatever our partnership had become. What if we'd just stayed in Edinburgh, doing what we had done for years? Writing, walking, laughing.

We had spent a strained afternoon divvying up jobs, so that we could speak as little as possible. I kept attempting terrible, cheesy jokes, ones that she'd usually laugh uproariously at, but her face remained rigid. I even made a joke about that – asked her where she'd got her Botox done – but nothing.

Over those awful weeks living apart, but still so close, we continued our usual Sunday night 'family meetings', as we'd called them for all these years, something sweet and functional copied from happily married heterosexual couples with kids on Pinterest.

It used to be that we would spend, say, thirty minutes working out who was where for their respective jobs and freelance work, what was happening the following weekend with our pals, who would walk Bruno each day, plan out our meals. It's weird the things you miss, isn't it?

Those meetings had instead become us going through our respective points on an agenda, perhaps passing over notes or documents, occasionally disagreeing or puzzling out how to match our next jobs together without talking. Our WhatsApp chat went from silly gifs and requests to pick up some choccie biccies on the way home to occasional thumbs-up reactions and single sentences with full-stops.

She'd been wearing her grey glasses. Her serious frames. Her depression frames.

We had agreed ages ago to appear on a podcast together, one called Whisky Witches. It seemed like a good idea at the time, just like the BBC documentary had. Any media to promote our project and all that.

I'd suggested we do it together from the office, that it might look weird if we were on Zoom from different places. But she just kept saying no.

I know a common suggestion is to set boundaries, to protect your boundaries, but more than once I have wondered how fair it is for someone to have a boundary that disregards the other person's needs.

I always thought I might do a podcast. It's a happy medium between blog and vlog, but I never found the confidence. Or, really, I know how judgemental I can be, so I was scared of opening up another route for people to criticise me – or me to criticise myself with what I assumed people were thinking about me. I can be quite derisive of other people's Instagrams or podcasts – I mean is a poetry Instagram really the best way to portray your art?

I remembered my book, how solid and real that felt. I could hold it in my hands, I could prove, for ever, that I had created something. The dream had come true – I had someone I could call my agent, my editor; I could drop it into conversations. Except, when it was published, it didn't live up to my dream. The sales were good, I suppose, for what it was, but they weren't life changing. All it meant was pressure to do more, say what was next, to write another book. And I couldn't do it, even with the encouragement of my editor. It remains, to this day, an unfinished project – my difficult second album. I had spent years writing my blog, and transformed all the best parts of it into a book – a book that broke me in the making of it, but was reviewed as average at best. My agent kept suggesting I branch out for a while, do YouTube, do more online: engage, engage, engage.

★

The women who made Whisky Witches, really, they did what I hoped I could do, but that made them all the easier to pick apart. Their whole schtick is that it's three women talking about whisky – yet it's still thick with masculinity. The segments are introduced by a deep-voiced man and interspersed with heavy rock riffs. Not that women can't like rock. I do get myself a bit mixed up with feminine versus masculine – I am trying to make the whisky sphere more inclusive to women but in doing so I often reduce us and men into stereotypes. I just find it strange that a female-led podcast is still leaning so heavily into the male. It remains my favourite one though, despite this wee gripe.

'Today we have Morag and Eilidh McIntyre, two women promising to disrupt the male-dominated industry. We've had Eilidh on before on our feature about women's impact on the industry, so go back to episode forty-three and take a listen after this, especially the bit about Bessie Williamson, the "first lady of Scotch" who, amongst other things, protected Laphroaig during the war.

'Now, if you haven't heard already, Morag and Eilidh have purchased Ardkerran Distillery in Campbeltown, a place that shut down in the eighties along with dozens of other distilleries in the whisky bust of that period. We have covered Springbank and Glen Scotia here before, and of course Springbank opened Glengyle to attempt to retain Campbeltown's status as a whisky region which, rightly or wrongly, was under threat.

'At one point, Campbeltown was hailed as "Whisky Capital of the World", even earning itself nicknames such as "Whiskyopolis" and "Spiritsville". It had just the right mix of elements in the nineteenth century: access to coal, peat, bere – a kind of rough barley – and soft water. Plus, there was even a time when a steamer boat went to Glasgow daily. Places like Speyside, however, benefited from the railway revolution where Campbeltown could not. There were once over thirty distilleries there, in the most remote mainland town in Scotland. There are many theories about the collapse of distilling in the area – nonetheless, the question of whether two or even three distilleries are enough to merit a "region", and if so whether more areas and islands should be given their own region status, is still a hot topic in the industry.

'But three more are opening up in the region over the next five years. Of course, we had to start with this one first. Not only is it an independent distillery, but it is the first women-owned distillery in Scotland. Tell us, what do you plan to do differently from the lads?'

My heart ached at Morag on the screen. She had Bruno beside her, leaning on her shoulder, occasionally putting his face in front of hers. It was adorable. I couldn't speak. I felt choked. She smiled and paused, perhaps waiting for me, then ploughed ahead.

'Well, first of all, thank you so much for having us on. We're both very big fans of yours.' That was a lie: she had never listened to an episode, even when we'd been on long driving trips. She prefers music to a podcast. 'I'll start with a stereotypically girly issue – skincare. While searching for how we can be more environmentally friendly, we came across a recent study that shows the discards of whisky can be used for skincare. For every hundred litres of whisky we make, we have enough of the probiotic barley and liquid remains to make ten jars of the stuff! We've already partnered with a soap-maker back in Edinburgh who's put together samples for us of an enriched day cream and is working with a technician from the whisky labs in Glasgow. Very exciting stuff. We'll be the first to take this study on board.'

'And, Eilidh, what about the process of the making of your whisky? What will you, what *are* you doing differently? Or, maybe, what have you learned from your time reporting on whisky that you'll be using here?'

'Well, we . . . I . . . Look, what has been shown time and time again is that women have a better nose. I have often hoped studies can be done to back this up, but, anecdotally, women often make better blenders. We now know more about why women might see more colours than men – having more cones or less of a propensity for colour blindness, for example – but we don't know why they might be able to, well, not only taste and smell more nuances but describe them better. You know Susan Lafferty? Some of my best memories are those spent with her, making up detailed tasting notes on the unusual or unique things to compare whisky to, like how beer tasting notes include "ironing board" as a point of comparison. Trust me, once you smell it, you'll know. Anyway, I think, not only all of that, but over the years women have had different frames of reference than men. I'm talking completely in generalisations, of course, and maybe it isn't so much better as different. If we've had a long time of whisky being a male-dominated industry, then they have become, I don't know, set in their ways? An echo chamber? And now more and more women are coming in and viewing – and smelling and tasting – things a bit differently, you know?'

I kept rubbing my nose and sniffing and clearing my throat loudly. A nervous habit that I hate when others do and so I hate myself even more when I do it. I placed my hands under my thighs before I continued.

'Something you've covered on your podcast before is the history of women in whisky, which you know is something we've discussed before, um, as you said, um, before, but . . . essentially, brewing used to be part of the women's work of the household. Even workplaces – even one of the hospitals in Glasgow – had their own stills, albeit illicit ones. So what I'm saying is, maybe we're not actually going to do anything new. But we will certainly remind everyone what women are capable of and have been capable of for so long.'

It works sometimes to not think, to just speak. Morag was still smiling. At the screen? At the other women? At Bruno nuzzling her cheek? At me?

'Lovely, and we so support that here at Whisky Witches. Have you already got a flavour profile in mind for your first distillation? Where are you on renovations? How soon can we expect the first bottling?'

Morag jumped in: 'I'll let Eilidh tell you about flavours, but regarding the refurbishment of the distillery, absolutely everything is going according to plan, and there have been, fingers crossed, no impediments to us getting our job done.' Another lie. She curled her hair behind both ears simultaneously. It's one of her nervous behaviours – she was saying something she'd rehearsed.

I checked she was finished before I went in. 'As for flavours, well, the area is known for some mild peat, some sea air finish, and I think for having quite a smooth movement down the back of the tongue and into the throat. I want to keep in with that tradition, but it's been really difficult to find peat. The other two distilleries here actually import it! Luckily, our distillery is somewhat outside the town in comparison and built out of old farmhouses, so we have some land here. I hope to use peat from nearby as much as possible, same with the barley, what with terroir being a burgeoning area of whisky-making, but also more of an emphasis on locally sourced products in general, but it's all taking a bit longer than I hoped. It's important to me that I do it right. That, uh, we do it right.'

'Excellent, of course. So tell us about you two. You've been together so long. Apart from perhaps Rita and Takeshi in Japan, you might also be the only business partners to do this as a couple. What's it like spending all that time together and how does being two people who know each other so well help you run a business? Will we be able to taste the love in every drop?'

They all tittered. Morag and I did not.

CHAPTER 21

Eilidh
2023

It was November, and I couldn't imagine darker weeks were yet to come.

Heather and her crew were back for their next round of filming, and our court date was looming. Unfortunately, the news of the injunction and the article full of venomous quotes had reached Heather. Of course it had. She is a dogged researcher and this would have jumped out straightaway in any search. She thought it would 'add excellent conflict' to the documentary. I managed not to snap back at that, that actually it had added 'awful conflict' to our lives, the lives of real human beings.

And Morag now had to be in so many shots with me – we didn't really get enough before – and of course we had to. The whole point was we were making this dream come true as a couple, together.

It reminded me of when we were first together, that first year especially, when even our knees touching sent that wave of frisson through me, where her smell seemed like a high, when even seeing her pick her nose when she thought I wasn't looking somehow made my heart go all a-flutter.

Except those tingles were always tinged with fear. Fear of what I might lose for ever, fear of how much I hated myself, fear of how she looked at me – even when she was smiling, I imagined I could see disgust beneath the glint and shine.

Stood next to her, I couldn't help but inhale her; even her raspberry shampoo – which I had been forbidden to touch since I once used half a bottle in one bath, probably because I wanted to douse myself in it so much – was intense. Over the years I had become desensitised to her smell – how had I let myself stop appreciating how good she smelled? Is that what happens after a decade together?

I couldn't tell if I was looking forward to the moment we filmed together or not. In front of Heather and the guys, we were almost ourselves. We riffed, we revived our in-jokes, we sometimes even linked arms. As soon as they left, however, it was like she went dark, turned into her shadow self. She was mean, even.

Like when we toured the parts we had finished – we overlapped each other in our excitement over the new kiln, black, heavy and iron, and with pipes and arms reaching into various rooms to load barley into and allow smoke to release from. We both skipped around the brand-new bottling room and squealed over the label printer and corker. We practically ran outside to show off our newly constructed peat shed – and then nothing. Like leaving a full Zoom meeting, the sound shut off all at once, and suddenly you're reminded how alone you are, with nothing but the screen light and an empty drinks can and a silent flat.

She didn't even say bye before she left that day.

There were some positives to the filming crew's intrusions. First, and Morag did agree, there's nothing like talking someone else through your project and how far you've come in such a short space of time to realise that, actually, you're doing a good job. Them leaving for a couple of months and seeing their reaction to our progress when they came back was cathartic. When you're in the trenches of a huge undertaking – be it something academic like a dissertation or physical like a great canvas of art or a tapestry – it is hard to see that each word, each brushstroke, each thread pulled and knotted, is one small part towards the final whole.

Second, Heather had sleuthed where I could not bear to – she had narrowed down who she believed the critics in the article were. I'm not sure of the ethics of journalism, and I wasn't in a place to ask Morag, but it sounded like Heather had done a lot of phoning around and asking, as a journalist, to 'follow up' what they had said in the *Courier* article, despite the fact that they had remained anonymous. Two people had fallen for this trick, a local couple called David and Lizzie.

Despite there being numerous churches in Campbeltown, built, somewhat controversially at the time, by the local whisky barons from their profits off the drink – perhaps as a way to offset their dabblings with what was seen by many as a gateway to sin – there were few believers left nowadays. David and Lizzie were two of them.

I think most people our age have religious trauma – especially queer people. I read somewhere that the generation or two younger than us are spiritually lost. Where we had something concrete to rebel against and root our identities in, as atheists or agnostics even, they have no grounding or guidance there, except the people they follow online, who they project a kind of religious parasocial fervour onto.

I try not to judge, I try to rationalise my antipathy to religious people – after all, there are angels and arseholes in every category and group – but my upbringing still cuts into my thoughts and, probably, my voice. I remember so clearly sitting in the pew next to my mother as a teenager, hearing the vicar talk about homosexuality being *against nature* – but not understanding why I felt weird and squirmy about it. I didn't realise at the time that the deep affection and intense fascination I had with some girls my age was anything more than friendly admiration.

I couldn't help but picture David and Lizzie as the worst kind of Christians – always looking down on, but never helping people up. Preaching things that Jesus never said. Oftentimes, in fact, the opposite.

This might sound strange, but when we first moved here, I went to a few of the churches. I sometimes seek that quiet certainty that being in church once gave me as a child. To me, it is an interesting marker of an area or community, to see what their church says they do, versus what they actually do. Several here have regular days and events simply to bring people together, to offer food and a warm space, a place to connect. There's one we even got flyers from – they were posted into the caravan, inviting us to their Christmas meals next month.

I felt watched as soon as I stepped into David and Lizzie's church, months before, when I didn't know who they were – perhaps it was simply because I was a stranger, but it felt more than that. Unwelcome. It was no secret that the two new whisky distillery owners were wife and wife. I wondered if it was just me, projecting my assumptions onto the congregation, but when Heather told me those two were behind some of the nasty quotes, my gut told me to trust it more: it had been right again.

And if I had religious trauma, what Morag had was worse. There was a point where her father even made her go to a 'special group for people like her' for a period as a teenager. It was, to all intents and purposes, conversion therapy, albeit light touch – a weekly 'chat' as a youth group, with tea and custard creams. As the years passed, as homosexuality became more visible and accepted in the mainstream, and perhaps as Morag grew into herself, her father stopped bringing up the possibility of her getting married to a man at all. They even became close, for a time. I never warmed to him, though.

When I asked his permission to marry her, he looked visibly sick. He didn't show this side of himself when Morag and I were together with her family. He reserved it for when we were in the room alone. Sometimes, he'd ignore me completely. Other times, he made a point of highlighting how much smarter he and Morag were than me, how much *history* and *heritage* his family had compared to mine. And that I was just a phase of Morag's, or else that I was after their money.

He actually didn't give me an answer that day – he told me he would think about it. I had already resolved the moment I left, fists clenched and talking angrily out loud to myself on the streets, that I would do it anyway. I would marry my love. Why did I even go to him in the first place? I had some weird thought that that was the only way to do it right, but that's not the world we live in anymore – he did not own his daughter. I can only assume Morag's mum talked him into it, because he called me the same evening, without a hello, and said: 'Fine, but you cannot get married in our church. I will pick out a suitable alternative for you.' And then he hung up.

So Heather's suggestion that we meet with David and Lizzie at a local café, have a conversation with them to see if we could bridge the gap, went down about as well as you'd expect.

It felt like we were two couples, at the end of a competitive reality TV show, like *Four in a Bed* or *Wife Swap*, about to face each other with some hard truths. What happened to keeping this documentary 'celebratory and light-hearted'?

The cameras didn't help – two, to capture as many angles of our discomfort as possible.

David and Lizzie looked righteous. Morag looked sick.

Her eyes kept flitting between the door and the counter. She swallowed her tea clumsily, in great gulps that ran down the sides of her mouth. I hadn't seen her like this before, probably not ever.

Should I have called it off right there and then?

Should I have placed my hand on her hand?

I was scared to.

Heather explained what was going to happen, that she would prompt us to speak and we should allow each other to finish.

My estimation of her went down. What was the purpose of the documentary she was making? I'd thought this was to be a sweet and informative piece charting Scotland's first women-owned whisky distillery, not some tacky reality show that feeds off of people's pain. Include our trials and tribulations, sure, but this?

I decided I wouldn't give them or her anything.

Lizzie started: 'We just think that we are acting in the best interests of our community.' Her smile was smug, her pale lipstick was smudged, and her hair was boring. As per Heather's instructions, I waited for Lizzie to finish – perhaps for David to add more – but that seemed to be it. Good, I was glad we were giving dead air. Hopefully this would all be unusable.

What did she mean by 'community'? What did she mean by 'our' community?

Morag was staring at the cash register, almost vacant. I was concerned she was somehow zoning out, that she wasn't coping with the situation at all. I didn't realise this would be so difficult for her.

David cleared his throat as if to speak – then stopped. It was painfully awkward. Heather went to add something, and us four collectively slowly swung our faces up towards her, as if to say, 'Yes, and?' I don't think they wanted to be here either.

Heather even looked a little flustered, but I caught Lizzie's eye and, somehow, we started giggling together. What a ridiculous situation.

'Look,' started Lizzie, flattening out her napkin onto the Formica table. 'This feels a bit bizarre and manufactured. We have nothing against you. Or what you're doing. Not at all. We just need to protect what's ours.'

I was incredulous at this. 'What's *yours*? What do you mean? If you want your name on our loans, you are certainly welcome to them!'

'No, no, no, it's not that. Look.'

Why did she start every other sentence with 'look'? It's like folk who say 'ultimately' as if to say their point of view is the only correct one, disregarding your own feelings and beliefs, like you're simply not looking hard enough at the reality of a situation.

It's weird the things that make my blood boil.

'Look,' she began again. 'We've had so many organis-ations, companies, come to this place and, well, make promises they couldn't keep. We don't know you, and well, look, maybe we should have come to speak to you before we filed an interdict against you but–'

'But what?' I think I shouted it, then I took a deep

breath to steady myself, to stay true to not giving the cameras anything.

'Well, it's not just us. It's a group of us – a group of twenty folk or more. We've been bitten too many times. Look, you know what they say, fool me once, shame on you . . .'

Morag carried on the saying, 'Fool me twice, shame on me. Yes, but, right, what are you saying? What have we ever done?'

I was glad Morag seemed to have come to the present a little more, that she had been listening, that her debating instincts were kicking in.

'Look, I know you read the article; Heather said so. We laid it all out there. The injunction really is to ensure everything, and I mean absolutely everything, is up to code, that everything is done properly. We want this to be a success – we want this to work – but it has to be done properly. The interdict was the only way to ensure it was, because, that way, every single element will be checked, and thoroughly. And I mean everything, down to every nail you hammer in, will be assessed. Too much of Campbeltown's future rests on this. We can't have any doubts that this business is flawless. The other distilleries are such a draw for tourists and the like, and we have barely hung onto our whisky region status – what if you ruined all of that?'

I sat agape. I still couldn't tell whether this was a good thing or not. I was never good under scrutiny. It's why I prefer not to have passengers when I drive. But it seemed for the greater good, somehow, that our being legally and thoroughly scrutinised means they cared we did well. Except all these extra folk in and out of our buildings as information was gathered for the case were adding an unnecessary stress – one which would be there even without the dead bodies.

David finally spoke, clearing his throat again before he did so. 'What we want is transparency. Forcing companies and whatever you are, entrepreneurs or something, to be so by using the law is the only way now. Do you know how many times we've got our hopes up by a new business, hopes that it will revolutionise this town, that our young people can feel proud again, be employed, only to be screwed over again? No, I stand by it. What Lizzie and I and the group have done was the only way.'

Morag replied: 'Right. How about you come to a meeting? At the distillery? Or someone from your group, Campbeltown Cares, why don't you come along and be a part of what we are making? You'll see. We're not perfect. We're just two women who care. We care too. We're not some big corporation coming in . . . We've chosen to live here, to make new lives here, and . . .'

We all turn to see what she is looking at over by the specials board – but there isn't anything.

She doesn't say another word before she gets up, takes off her lapel mic and leaves.

The cameras are still rolling. I try to make sense of what the couple in front of me are saying.

'So what you're saying is, you've added all this extra stress and worry and, you know, delay, to our honest, real business and dream, just so you can have legal documentation that everything is up to code? That we aren't here to scam some government grants, that we will actually leave the place better than we found it? Or, well, that we'll stay and be its caretakers?'

Lizzie and David looked at each other, and then nodded at me.

'And do you intend to continue with this?'

David cleared his throat again. 'How about we come to that meeting Morag suggested? Then we can report back to the group, maybe see what has been gleaned about your distillery renovations so far, and we can all talk again.'

It was all I could hope for at that point. I should have been angry, although I could understand their motives in that roundabout 'for the greater good' kind of way, but my rage was eclipsed by my concern over Morag.

I left them my number, refused to acknowledge Heather and tried to follow Morag, but I was too late. She was not on the route home, she was not up any side streets or alleyways, she was not anywhere that I could find her in the radius of the café. She just . . . disappeared.

I stood at the water's edge, breathing heavily, staring, not into the distant hills across the sea, but down, down into the churning foam hitting the stones below.

It felt like there was nothing I could do to repair Morag and me. In my head, the only thing that made sense was resolving everything I could, proving to Morag that we had nothing to worry about with the bodies. I couldn't get rid of them, but I could get rid of the weight of them.

I returned to the Aladdin's Cave, to take stock of where I was, to continue unravelling the mystery, the cold case murder on our hands. I vowed to stay all night if I had to.

I returned to some of the names I had before and searched all through the documents and kept entering different variations of a name followed by 'disappearance Campbeltown' into Google.

By 2 a.m., I had hundreds of tabs open, three finished cans of energy drink and a disarray of crumpled old papers around me.

And that's when I found it: 'TWO LOCAL MEN LOSE THEIR LIVES IN CAMPBELTOWN LOCH'.

It was short, only part of a column really, but there they were: the faces of the two dead men, but alive, in the warehouse surrounded by barrels. The article explained that Alistair and Duncan had been missing for two days before their boat was found, unmoored and drifting, with smashed glasses and empty whisky bottles aboard.

That was it – in August 1971 – these two men, whose bodies were never found, were proclaimed drowned at sea. Drunk. It was more of a warning to others of the dangers of drink than a compassionate piece about two people who had lost their lives. It didn't even mention that they worked at the distillery despite the selected image – but I knew they did.

I walked up the stairs as delicately as I could manage and glimpsed through the gap in the door to check Morag was in the office. Bruno was asleep on top of a lump of blankets but that's all I could see. For a moment I imagined she had found someone else's bed to sleep in and I felt a twang in my chest. With the door pushed open in tiny increments, I finally revealed one of her hands, hanging from the edge of the sofa, and I skipped back to the caravan, suddenly elated.

I bookmarked the page of Alistair and Duncan, and slept in till past ten the following morning.

★

After that, I began to visit the Drookit Dug regularly. For company, perhaps. What else was there to do with my evenings? And in there I was a celebrity of sorts. I could put on my funny facade and tell stories. I could show off my whisky expertise, imply to all gathered that I was intelligent, especially coupled with my knowledge of philosophers and other interesting thinkers that I had gathered over the years. I had spent a considerable chunk of my twenties researching what I assumed was learned at private schools: Greek mythology and the pantheon of gods, pithy Latin sayings, Roman leaders and their respective lives and deaths, key characters and plot points of all the Shakespeare plays. All for no other reason than to *seem* smarter.

I often took Bruno too, which elevated my popularity further – who wouldn't want to come and say hello to the owner of the soft-eyed, waggy-tailed black Lab? Bruno was the kind of dog who would go home with a stranger if they showed him even a bit of affection – no loyalty. Or, rather, loyalty to everyone.

By the time December was underway, we were still waiting to hear whether our court hearing was to go ahead, whether Lizzie and David and their group had been satisfied by our tour and meeting on site. I had also tried every seat in the pub by that point. For an experiment, you know? Testing the feng shui, finding the optimal spot. If no one talked to me, or it was dead, I had my books to read or my phone to research on. I read more in those few weeks than I ever had.

It was even better when one or all of my newfound friends came in: Rob, Linksy, Bunty and Sheena. Sometimes it was all four, the former three being fully retired. Sheena's topic of conversation, particularly after her third Merlot, would often turn to the fact that she might never have such a luxury. Who would buy her business? That was her retirement, there, in the smokehouse. She'd tried putting it on the market a few years ago, and then again a couple of years after that. No one was buying here, and no one wanted to buy a business here. At this point, Bunty usually started buying the rounds of drinks, perhaps as a way to apologise for her own financial independence. After a while, I noticed she favoured the same green cardigan over everything, and she'd pull it tighter to her, like a protective cocoon. We often played cards – those were the best nights, where we could grow closer through competition and friendly insults. Rob knew all the best card games and even taught me cribbage which was strangely addictive. I kept thinking back to all the times Morag and I travelled with a pack of cards, how one of our favourite things about going somewhere new was teaching or learning new games. But no more. I only saw her when it was pre-arranged, to discuss the renovation.

And during my increased time at the pub, I grew closer to Donald. The first few times he would always ask after Morag, but then he stopped. My responses about her were always airy and bright, but always brief. Perhaps he could sense trouble in paradise.

My favourite two spots were at the bar and in the corner by the fire. By the fire, I could pretend I had chosen to be in the pub, that I was drawn there as a romantic place to read, not that I had nowhere else to go. By the bar, I could guarantee a conversation with Donald, at least, if not an opportunity to tell raucous stories with locals and tourists alike. By then, the sun was setting by half past three in the afternoon, and I felt the compulsion to leave the caravan as soon as the light began to dim.

One evening, when I was feeling particularly morose, and therefore particularly cheered up by Donald's presence in comparison, he came and sat on my side of the bar. It was just us two in there. Bruno was asleep on his bobbled blanket, and we talked and talked and talked.

I don't know who started it, but soon we were touching. Our knees touched. Then our hands patted and stroked each other's legs and arms as punctuations to our sentences.

And then we kissed.

CHAPTER 22

You
2013

You stand on the esplanade, watching the boats bob in place, tracing the arcs of the dark birds overhead. This is a breeze unlike any other, and you've stood on many a coastline on many a continent.

It is the first time you have been back in Campbeltown for nearly three decades.

You remember swinging over and under these black painted railings as a child, as a teen, even sometimes as an adult. You're sixty-four now. Neither your grip strength nor your knees are what they once were. You think you can count the layers of flaked paint as the years that have passed since then, like rings on a tree stump.

Your mother has died. Your brothers have grandchildren now, and anyway they were never very good with anything like this, with the organisation and determination and compassion it takes to sort these things out. You're delaying walking to the house. You're trying to decide what to do next.

It's time, maybe. Time to come back, to settle down. To come home.

No one has recognised you so far, and from your superficial enquiries, half of them are dead now anyway. Hugh's son runs a local bar, but Hugh and his wife passed away within three months of each other a couple of years ago apparently. He died of a classic case of a broken heart, they said. She died of a classic case of breast cancer, not caught soon enough because there are no decent facilities here. As the Eider duck flies, Glasgow isn't even forty miles away. But it's hours away by car.

It happened a while ago anyway, that you turned invisible. Once, all it took was narrowing your eyes or touching your lips with your fingers or laughing in exactly the right way, and you had them in the palm of your hands. Now you're just another old person.

It's easier than you think, easy enough even to register at the local doctor's again – not that there are any spaces left at the dentist's – but at least you can get your thyroid pills just fine.

Easy enough to pretend, as you clear out your mother's house, as you stand at the funeral with only two other people, as you pick up your daily paper to give these old legs a stretch, to pretend to be someone else.

CHAPTER 23

Eilidh
2023/2024

Hogmanay. At ours.

What was I thinking? I'd just piled more jobs on top of both me and Morag. She barely reacted. Maybe I wanted to see how she'd react. I'd got swept up in things again, not considering the consequences of my own actions. Plus, the Campbeltown Cares group had, finally, with only hours to spare before we all had to appear in court, decided to drop the injunction against us. It was a welcome relief, not least because the lawyer we had found to help us appeal it seemed inept at best (though very affordable), but now we could, maybe, enjoy the process of our renovation. Sort of. I had fantasised that me and Morag would jump into each other's arms with the weight of it all magically melted away, but she was still quite business-like and brusque with me.

More than that, I felt guilty about what had happened with Donald and I wanted to do something practical, something to take my mind off it. He'd seemed to want to pretend it hadn't happened too.

When Sheena told me Victoria Hall was shut for its first winter since 2020, and before that no one in living memory could remember it being closed, I couldn't help but offer our malting floors.

They weren't being used yet anyway, and on a tour of one of the other Campbeltown distilleries I'd seen their strings of fairy lights and listened wide-eyed as they told us about the room once being filled with market stalls for Christmas. I imagined the long low-roofed rooms filled with disco lights and bumping bass. A great wobbly oval of people holding hands and running in and out to 'Auld Lang Syne' at the bells.

I imagined I could manufacture a meet-cute, where Morag and I would have to clasp hands as we danced in groups and she wouldn't be able to deny the connection we still had, that there was something still there to nurture. That I could erase what I had done with Donald. I didn't even like it – I didn't even want him. I just wanted her.

I was surprised at how many people accepted the invite on Facebook. Hundreds. Could we even fit that many? I wasn't sure how legal it was, and I wasn't about to check. Ask for forgiveness and not permission has always been one of my mottos.

All we asked for was three quid on the door, to pay for the leccy and lights. A local lad offered his ridiculously over the top sound system if he could DJ and, yes, we were pretty sure it was big enough for the space. Another guy, a high school physics teacher working way past retirement age, said his ceilidh band would play if they could each be guaranteed some of the first bottles of our whisky. I knew they'd drink it too, savour it, tell the tale of our distillery, us bringing it back from the brink, that they wouldn't just keep it to sell on later. We'd already debated having a 'one bottle per customer' policy, like other distilleries sometimes have to do, so that our whisky remained in the hands of people who could enjoy it, and the price wouldn't rocket wildly online, benefiting only the seller and a select few collectors who could afford it, at the exclusion of everyone else. When Morag and I had been blue-sky thinking about the distillery, when it had been a mere pipe dream, before we even thought about raising money to buy it, we had agreed this should be our policy. Whisky as currency is not what we wanted; we wanted our whisky to be enjoyed, to be shared, to be treasured.

Part of me also hoped our Hogmanay event would not only be a way to curry favour with the locals, whose good books we seemed to now be in, but to do some further digging. An innocent question inserted here and there. An appraisal of the crowd. Morag and I hadn't discussed how we would arrange ourselves, but I had assumed what she would say – we circle, we host, we keep busy and away from each other.

Surprisingly, we were further along in the renovations than we thought possible, especially considering the limitations imposed by the injunction, and I wondered what we could achieve now they were lifted. I mean, we were not quite on track with her Gantt chart, but since we'd been dividing and conquering, and since I had decided the best way to gain her trust again was to do exactly as she told me to do – while concealing my continued research into the murders – we had progressed wonderfully well. I was even starting to believe that I had, indeed, been the problem.

I had even hired our very own coppersmith – an extremely rare find, but they had just finished their apprenticeship with Diageo and wanted to go somewhere smaller, somewhere more independent. Plus, Atlas, the coppersmith, told me they tried to fit in with the other apprentices – all male – but the lads didn't quite know how to square the concept of non-binary with their understanding of the world.

Atlas showed off their dark red nail varnish and bejewelled nose-bridge piercing on the camera during their interview and I got it. We swapped stories of gender presentation revelations during the pandemic and agreed they'd start very soon. That's another thing we'd progressed with – the housing.

So many distilleries across Scotland are rural – in several cases the towns sprang up around them, rather than them being founded in places already populated. We wanted to offer affordable housing here, and this was an opportunity Atlas wouldn't get in many other places – although coppersmiths are highly sought after and they could have, potentially, gone anywhere. We had converted one long building into three living spaces – think twee Airbnbs – each with a bedroom, kitchen-cum-living room and a bathroom. I'll give credit to Morag for those – she'd corralled the builders so well. I caught her too, once, working in the middle of the night, by the light of our old camping lantern, sanding and painting. All the roofs on all the buildings that we were allowed to touch were finally fixed too, although, upsettingly, that caused more problems since it turned out you needed the roofs off in order to remove and replace mash tuns and larger pieces of equipment, and we will kick ourselves forever for that oversight – but that was a problem for another time. It still felt like two steps forward and one step back, which was progress of some kind at least.

I'd also hired a few people to work the kiln and mash tuns and copper stills, once they were completed, but most of them already lived in or around the town. Most of them hadn't had a job in years or at all. Sourcing some of the new equipment (or, rather, old: acquired from distilleries upgrading during this current whisky boom) was the most fun I'd had in ages – I actually forgot all about the mystery of the bodies for a whole week. The old mash tuns were still there. Manky and rotted and full of festering water. I had hoped there wouldn't be any further surprises in the depths beneath the thick layer of scum.

★

The first hour of the Hogmanay party was fairly tame, fairly dead, and somehow Morag was always facing away from me, no matter where I moved to in the malting room.

She'd done a superb job with the place – long tables laden with picky bits from Tesco along one wall (I made sure to collect exactly what was on the list she gave me, and no more or less), a stage marked out in duct tape for the band and DJ at one end, and wee collections of tables and chairs at the other end, covered in jars of fresh flowers and jugs of water.

By 7 p.m., the place was heaving. Hot. I was soon invited by two absolute strangers to dance the Dashing White Sergeant with them. Then, my group and Morag's joined hands for a circle of eight one way, then the next. She couldn't change places fast enough, and we were holding hands, touching, for the first time in weeks.

I gave her a squeeze that she didn't return.

By the time her group met with mine again, she had moved into the middle so it wouldn't happen again. I could still smell her perfume, though. Somehow it made my eyes sting and I had to blink and wipe at my eyes in between my pas de basque.

At the end of the song, I thanked my two new friends, whose sweat-soaked underarms made me feel better about my own, and retreated to the edges to observe and surveil the crowd before me. Synonyms flooded my mind as I attempted to embody a ruthless, calculating and astute spy. Who was mingling? Who was sitting? And why?

Sheena, her usually sharply cut hair pinned back for the occasion, appeared to choose alternate songs to dance to. Her mascara was smudged, but she looked unfazed – radiant even. Rob stayed sat down the entire time, banging one of his wide flat hands off his thighs and knees in time with the music, while the other hand remained constantly preoccupied with placing pints and drams and pizza slices into his mouth. Linksy, as ever, was more of a talker than anything else, and moved from group to group to insert himself and his stories in the middle. Bunty, poor thing, looked done in after just one dance. Donald had helped with the set-up but was nowhere to be seen.

The skirts swirled for the Canadian Barn Dance, and everyone laughed at the occasional claps hit out of time; the Gay Gordons back and forth made me recall the struggles Morag and I have had over the years working out who is better as the partner at the back; the slower, more intimate, St Bernard's Waltz elicited a few tears from me. Every time the dancers raised up onto their toes, I had to sniff deeply to call the tears back.

Then I found I couldn't watch anymore, so I rushed away to the food tables, eyeing up a few of the older folk as people I could surreptitiously query about their lives and their local knowledge.

That's when Donald arrived, back from wherever he'd been – wearing the exact same appalling tartan suit as the dead men.

My heart lurched – through guilt over what had happened the other day or through fear, I couldn't say.

Was it the lighting? Was it *definitely* the same awful suit?

I was frozen in place.

He walked straight for me, hand raised in a wave, but I couldn't hear what he was saying.

With every step, the likeness between him and the third man in the picture wearing the tartan suits grew.

The same nose. The same peppery beard that only

recently had been scratching my face. The exact same tartan suit.

Linksy had said it was his father.

What if it was his dad who did it? What if he knew what his dad did and he was here, now, allowing me to become entwined with him to protect his father's secret at any cost?

The lights pulsed and became too much. The thin room seemed even thinner.

I knocked a plate from someone's hand and I think I shouted an apology at them before I ran outside.

I leaned on the damp mossy wall, knees bent, arms on my shins, like some mock forward fold. I tried to gulp, but a strong gust of wind filled my mouth and for a moment I couldn't breathe.

No one came to find me.

I stood in misery, tears flowing down my face, choking back any noise. This is why Morag doesn't cry, I think. It's too much. Feelings overwhelm.

I tried to count ten red things I could see around me to calm down.

One, rust on the drainpipe. Two, a set of Christmas lights strung around a house in the distance. I spent some time watching a russet-coloured ladybird, three, wondering how it was there when frost spiked from the pipe like the remnants of blackheads on a nose strip, feeling my diaphragm slow and loosen. Four, the blood from the skin around my thumb I'd been worrying into a tear for days. Five, flames, licking the warehouse.

I was still searching for my sixth thing when I did a cartoonish double-take – fire!

I was torn as to whether to run back in and alert everyone or investigate for myself. Shit, shit, shit.

I decided on the latter and ran towards the warehouse.

The fire was in the exact corner where the barrels resided.

Just as I was standing, watching the conflagration rise from a mere metre to several metres high right above me, the fierce heat stinging my cold nose, something hard hit me on the back of the head.

CHAPTER 24

You

2023/24

The girls have been at the distillery since August, but this is the first time you've had a good chance to look around in years. You run your hands along the rough brick walls of the malting room, where it all began for you as a child, sweeping and scooping and turning barley.

It's not really changed.

Like the hills and the trees and the burns which alter with seasons yet remain the same solid constants in your landscape.

The last ten years back here in Campbeltown have gone by uneventfully enough. You've been doing all the things you've wanted to do for so long – spending hours reading uninterrupted, learning to bake, taking long walks in the style of Nan Shepherd with only your internal monologue and slowly detangling emotions, which you have repressed for so long, for company. You've even been experimenting with homebrewing in your airing cupboard – first wine, then gin, and now whisky. That is the only thing missing really – the distillery. You've sometimes walked past it, more to check that it is still shut or as a way, like a photograph might, to jog your memories.

But now it's open again. You've tried to ingratiate yourself somewhat – tried to make it look helpful or like an accident. You could tell straight away that Morag was the shrewder of the two, so trusting wee Eilidh became your target to befriend, to manipulate. Not that you've ever had a plan, just do what you can to remove the bodies or . . . something.

You can't be sure, but you suspect. You think she knows about the bodies, but does she know that you know?

You first glimpsed them at the pub. Eilidh led such a fine tasting you wondered if she'd read your own notes. She burned with the same passion for whisky you have. You almost feel bad for what she has inherited from you. But tonight is the perfect excuse to find the barrels again, to ascertain whether they have been disturbed after all these long years.

You bring your three pounds, a bottle of homebrewed wine, and wear an outfit that was once just the right amount of too tight, but now hangs off your frame. Your once strong and bulging arms have become straight and a little wobbly. Maybe a lot wobbly.

The party is in full swing once you arrive – that was the plan anyway, to slip in among them all, watch from afar.

You almost have fun – the girls know how to throw a party. And who can resist a sausage roll? Especially when they're the wee ones, and you can kid yourself you've barely had any when you've probably eaten the equivalent of three normal-sized ones.

Ceilidh dancing is something else. Strangers clasping hands, girls dancing with girls and boys with boys if the occasion calls for it, with not much of a fuss. Even when the caller is drowned out, everyone feels the count of eight in their hearts and the repetitive swirls and polkas and pas de basque flow and continue on, the room perfectly in unison. You step in for the Dashing White Sergeant – it's easy to join an existing couple to make a three – and although you're out of breath by the third or fourth set, you power through till the end of the dance, and all the ceilidhs from your past coalesce and meet with this one.

That one dance is plenty, but you do recall a time where you refused to sit out even one, even for a sneaky cigarette round the back.

You see the way Eilidh and Morag are at such cross-purposes – Eilidh desperately trying to catch Morag's eye and Morag fervently attempting to avoid it. What is happening with them?

Just as you're reaching for your fifth or maybe eighth wee sausage roll, Eilidh sprints past you, knocking your plate all down you. It lands with a clatter to the floor. You do not pick it up.

You decide it's the perfect excuse to follow her.

She stands outside, holding her sides tightly.

Ignoring the warm squelch of stovies slipping down your front, you stand as still as you can in the shadows as you watch her cry.

You remember standing here, before, decades ago, as a child.

You remember standing here, before, decades ago, as a young adult in their first job.

You remember standing here, just the other month, after you visited the girls in their caravan on the pretence of welcoming them to the area.

The shard of guilt and fear has been growing in your chest and now it hurts too much.

You have to get rid of the evidence, whether or not the girls have found them.

You're certain the whisky within all those casks, some of which you helped create, will help feed a fire so large it will destroy everything inside.

Maybe the barrels will even explode.

CHAPTER 25

Eilidh

2024

I woke up in a strange place. My body felt too heavy to move but all I could see was a spinning ceiling when I opened my eyes and so I felt that I had to move.

'Shh, no, no, keep still. Babe, it's okay, you've been in an accident.'

A stream of tears flowed from my eyes and my nose but I kept my eyes closed. I could feel Morag blotting my cheeks and stroking my forehead.

That's when I noticed the pain. Pain in my head. Pain in my leg. I tried to sit up again.

'No! Stay lying down. Please.' There was something in her voice I hadn't heard for so long – feeling.

Swallowing was difficult, thick, but I managed a croaky, 'What's, what's happened?' Lights were dancing in front of my eyes. But I was fairly sure they were still closed.

'There was a fire.' Her voice returned to sounding as serious as it had for the previous few weeks. 'The police are investigating . . . investigating the warehouse.'

I really wanted to, but I didn't try to sit up again.

'And we found you near it. We don't know what happened, but . . . they might have to transfer you to Glasgow or Fort William. They've already done X-rays of your leg and stitched you up as best they could, but . . . they haven't told me the extent of the damage yet.'

I asked for water and painkillers, and Morag helped me take them from my awkward lying-down position. As much as I hoped my injuries were not too severe, I couldn't help but feel an intense rush of emotion towards her, and I wished I was at least hurt enough for her to look after me for a little while.

I laughed to myself and snorted bubbles from my nose.

'Ugh, Eilidh.' She giggled. 'You're bubbling blood, you know.'

Her giggle. I vowed then to never faff about again. I told her so.

'Ahaha, don't make promises you can't keep. You know I consider it part of my daily job to scoop out the crumbs you leave behind in the margarine? To close all the drawers and cupboard doors you leave hanging open in your wake. Your mind is so often elsewhere, or maybe in different places, I don't think you can ever be a non-faffer.'

'You're right.' I coughed again. 'I reckon I hold the world record for Most Times "Mambo No. 5" Has Got Stuck In Anyone's Head.'

'I bet you do. What song is happening right now?'

I rootled around in my brain for the constant layers of noise it usually has, but it was fuzzy.

Just then, I heard a noise at the door. My eyes felt less sticky than they had a few moments before – from the tears or because I was more lucid, I do not know, but I wrenched them open and pulled them back as tightly as I could to take in the scene.

I was in a hospital, of sorts. There was a nurse at the foot of the bed with two mugs, steam curling from the top.

'I've brought you some hot choccies. Take this in and you'll feel better.'

She placed them on the table next to me and, without me really registering, managed to take my temperature, count my pulse and place a blood pressure cuff on me, seemingly in one swift movement.

I stayed in overnight, and by the dark morning I was more coherent. At least my head didn't feel so full of wet sand and neither did my eyes. Morag was asleep in the plastic chair next to me when I woke. I rolled onto my side, placed my hands in a prayer position underneath my left ear, then took the opportunity to stare. My injured leg protested, but I ignored it.

Morag's glasses were still on her face but had slipped down to the perilous tip of her nose. Her chin rested on her chest and her arms were squeezed tightly beneath her boobs. She was making no noise at all. I searched out the mole on her jawline, just under the bone of her neck, the one that I used to pluck the hair from every few weeks between the nails of my thumb and forefinger, just as she did to the random long white hair I get above my right eye.

I fucking love her.

If life is this, if all it is is plucking errant hairs from each other's faces, I want to be with her for it.

The song playing in my head at that moment, for some reason, was 'Baby Cakes'.

Someone cleared their throat at the foot of my bed. I jolted so badly I whacked the drip machine I didn't remember being attached to.

It was Donald. Large. Still in his tartan suit. I think my mouth opened and closed in a perfect impression of a goldfish. I still couldn't pull myself up. I felt more vulnerable than perhaps I had in my whole life, even more than when I asked Morag to marry me, even more than when someone mugged me and stole my tips on my way home from a shift at the restaurant. I gripped the sides of the bed with as much strength as I could muster in my weakened state.

'Are you feeling okay? We found you bleeding out into the mud and we–'

'What? You what?' I felt confrontational all of a sudden, like a creature backed into a corner.

He shrugged and sat on the end of the bed. I did my best to slide my leg inward, away from him. He looked . . . hurt?

'A beam fell and hit you on the head. You'd fallen over into some of the empty barrels outside. They'd rolled onto you. It was so frightening, like. Or they'd fallen into you. Anyway. I know you're not in a state to take all this in, really, but me and Morag have been talking. I have something to tell you.'

Then I really wanted to sit up. He seemed to sense it and pulled a gadget from a slot in the side of the bed.

'This changes the position of the bed – d'ye want me to help you sit up?'

I nodded. He clicked a few buttons and the half of the bed under my torso slanted upwards and upwards. He kept checking in, till I was finally at a position I was happy in.

I crossed my arms over my chest, one hand on each shoulder, like a vampire in a coffin, and tapped alternately on each collarbone, twice on the left side and once on my right – a trick I already knew for calming myself down that was reconfirmed when I finally joined TikTok in the long days of the lockdowns. The amount of tactics I learned over the years for myself, or coping strategies that somehow I worked out or tried and tested without even knowing, before I was ever diagnosed with anything – well, it was always strangely very reassuring when I learned they were genuine, recommended even.

I stopped tapping and motioned with my hand for him to continue. My mouth was dry again, and my throat was sore. You don't notice swallowing till you can't.

'My dad had the same ring.' He pulled the wee table on wheels over my bed and placed the two identical rings on it.

'Morag found this one in your pocket when you were brought here and I borrowed it. So I did some digging through old boxes of stuff my dad had. Morag showed me the photographs you found before.'

Morag snorted awake at her name and leaned forward ever so slightly – hesitant or restraining her excitement? She gave me a quick reassuring smile before she remembered herself and arranged a nondescript look on her face again.

He pulled out the photograph of the group at the front of the distillery gates. He pointed to the man in the beard, the man wearing a tartan suit like the one he was wearing.

'That's my dad. Hugh. This is his suit. I found a few photographs from the same time period, but – well, it looks like my mum's writing – someone has written names on these. Morag said you've been obsessing over the distillery history, and I thought I could help.'

I looked over at Morag for support, and she gave me another wee smile. I searched her eyes for the layers of disdain that had been present for the weeks before, and I couldn't find them. I took the photographs from Donald's hands and leafed through them, and he added some details, some names and locations we didn't know before.

When I reached one of the mystery woman, he cleared his throat and went to speak.

He stopped. I waited. Impatiently. He didn't continue.
'Yes?'

'Red hair. There was a woman who used to come round our house a lot. Um. I remember. I remember when I was a bairn. A woman sometimes came round for tea. And she didn't leave. I remember seeing her sometimes, in the morning. I never slept well, you see. Used to wake up before everybody else. And I'd see her, making a cuppa tea, or something. I didn't think it was weird at the time, but now . . . Aye, she'd stay over sometimes.'

Long red hair. Surely that's only one piece of the puzzle

– red hair is rare enough, even in Celtic countries, but that can't mean it is the same woman.

'What was her name?'

'Julia. Julia Murray.'

Did my eyes widen? Or were they still too heavy to betray my emotions? He wasn't to know my interest was more than just a casual curiosity about the history of my business, that I was attempting to track down a murderer, with almost no information, and from so long ago. He had given me an actual name to follow. And a woman's name, to match the woman's blouse covered in blood. It felt familiar – I was itching to return to the distillery to hunt her out, to find her among the distiller's reports and such.

'Morag told me you'd been looking for answers. She needed a confidante, I think, and she knew that you and I had been spending lots of time together. I think you find it easier to make pals.'

I tried to nod, but my head simply lolled from side to side. It's something that made us such a good pairing. I am fearless in my approaches with new people and new situations – more because I forget there would be any reason to do otherwise, than anything else – and she is quiet and calculating: not in a Machiavellian way, but in an anxious way. We had always balanced each other out. Yin and yang. She slows me down; I speed her up.

'Tell me about the rings.' I realised that 'r' sounds were hard on my tongue and mouth.

'My dad – Hugh McLafferty his name was – worked at Ardkerran. I'm not sure what he did – something to do with the barrels though, after the liquid was put through all the machines and that, I think. He was a Freemason – see the compass.'

I picked up one of the rings and held it very close to my good eye. The sharp points of the compass were clearer with this new information – what I thought was a stylised 'V' was actually a mathematical tool.

Another clue? Perhaps. I dug around in my memory for what I knew about the organisation, but all that came to mind was something to do with the Illuminati controlling the world, or some such nonsense. I doubt that kind of power had reached as far as here.

But I had more to go on now, more threads to pull – Freemasons, Hugh and Julia. I still wasn't sure whether I could trust Donald, but keeping him close couldn't hurt.

CHAPTER 26

Eilidh
2024

'Fair fa' your honest, sonsie face,
Great Chieftain o' the puddin-race!
Aboon them a' ye tak your place,
Painch, tripe, or thairm:
Weel are ye wordy of a grace
As lang's my arm.'

Donald brought in the haggis, round and plump on the plate, piped in by a local hobby bagpiper in full gear – kilt, sporran with tassels, socks with flashes and his sgian-dubh, the small dagger placed into the top of one sock. Donald placed the plate in front of Rob, who continued to recite Robert Burns's 'Address to a Haggis' before plunging the knife in and slitting along its body lengthwise, releasing a great plume of steam.

We'd already heard 'To a Mouse', my favourite, and an excerpt of 'Tam O' Shanter', a tale of drunkenness and witches. It is interesting how much of classic Scottish poetry is to do with drunkenness. I remember studying Hugh MacDiarmid in my undergrad – his epic 'A Drunk Man Looks at the Thistle' is on first glance a bit of nothing, but it is one of the deepest and most complex pieces of writing I have ever had the fortune to meet. Not that I appreciated it till someone, my professor, showed me the way. I am very glad I actually showed up to that particular seminar.

It was Burns Night, and we were hosting a Burns supper. There were three long tables in the room above the malting room, a cavernous space which would soon house piles and piles of barley. We cleared out the dust and the mice to the best of our ability, but as I sat there, I spied all the hanging tendrils of cobwebs we'd missed. I thought it would be a shame to get rid of them; they added a little something to the old feeling of the place. They made me imagine how many people over how many years had spent time in this room, whether as part of such a convivial occasion as this or not. One person told me their great-great-grandmother, or perhaps it was great-great-great, was born in this room, back when it was still a working farm.

The barley, once it had done drying and steeping, would rest up here, to eventually be loaded onto the bucket conveyor belt towards the kiln. Our malting floor was full of fresh barley. Our first batch. And we had hired a local wordsmith to recite our Burns for us, in among the keen locals who had vied for a few poems in between hers and her retelling of the life of Rabbie Burns. He had twelve children by four women, which I'm still not sure how I feel about, but he was known to be a charismatic soul, and one who highlighted the beauty in the bucolic, the communion between humanity and nature.

Forty people lined these three long tables. They had all either been invited or paid a modest sum to partake in this very Scottish ritual of ours. The number included a lot of Americans and Canadians, keen to experience their heritage.

It had been nearly a month since the fire and something – or, and I couldn't shake this feeling, *someone* – hit me on my head and crushed my leg. No one else seemed to suspect foul play, so I kept my awareness of what happened filed away for myself. The fire was blamed on an errant celebratory cigar, and my head and leg were collateral damage from the falling beams and barrels. I sensed from the police that they didn't care enough to investigate much, but that suited us.

I still used my crutches now and then, but on most days my left leg could bear the weight and just about bend tighter than ninety degrees. Miraculously, I was the most damaged thing there. Yes, of course our warehouse needed repairs, but in the grand scheme of all the work we still had left to do, it hadn't suffered too much harm. All the barrels remained unscathed.

And Morag and I had spent almost every waking hour together since, at least the ones during which she wasn't busy. She didn't sleep with me in the caravan, but she sat with me during the days, on the banquettes or the edge of the bed, looking guilty as hell. We were in a circle of guilt – her feeling ashamed of how thoroughly she had rejected me for all these weeks, and at how injured I was, even though I told her over and over again there was nothing she could have done differently, that the harm that had befallen me wasn't her fault. And there was my guilt at her guilt, knowing I was the one who had kissed someone else.

Every morning, she gently chapped on the caravan door, carrying another armful of treats to make me feel better: crisps, chocolate, magazines, puzzle books, notebooks and pens. Every lunchtime, she would come back with freshly made soup and thickly buttered bread, and she would update me on the day's progress. Every day, I would think this was it, this would be the day she found out what Donald and I had done.

What if she already knew?

I had become her latest project and I loved it. I loved when she, only half-jokingly, fed me soup and our eyes met and occasionally I spluttered the hot soup back at her as we giggled at the situation. I loved every time she replaced the bandages on my head. The moments when she parted and stroked my hair to inspect and clean my wounds were the most beautiful, the most tender, of them all.

I could pretend we were in a cheesy romance, where the nurse falls in love with their patient.

And this night, the twenty-fifth of January, our Burns supper, I pretended we were us again. That everything was on track.

It was the first reveal of our whisky. Not our own make, but the blends of what had been left behind.

While Morag dipped in and out to check up on me, I

spent the whole of January hobbling on my crutches with the copper valinch in hand taking small nips from various barrels to make our first bottlings. It would be more than three years before our first new-make whisky could be officially called Scotch or Scottish whisky – to earn such a designation, it must have been matured for three years and a day in an oak barrel. Till then, we were following the model of Bruichladdich, and others, of offering several small bottlings or batches, each one with a unique selling point or story of some kind.

Thus, the three on offer that night were:

1. Extra peaty – 'Ase Puckle', meaning the spark of a fire – partly made to cater to the Laphroaig-lovers of this world, who think being able to handle something so cough-inducing means that clearly they are the most manly of men, and partly made to cover up the intense iodine, provenance unknown, but assumed to be because of the sea air which infiltrates the dunnage warehouse. Like many whisky bottles, its label featured a beautiful landscape; this one was of a vista of the Campbeltown Loch except displayed in neon colours, with the surrounding sea and hills aflame.

2. A mixture of old and new – 'Bhuidseach Deoch', a way of saying a witch's brew or witchcraft potion – twenty per cent of a 1976 married with eighty per cent of a 1985, the latter of which was moved into new wood in the start of November, an act which Heather and her team had caught on film. Just a few weeks in a new cask, and it made all the difference; the sugars of the newly charred wood pulled the bitterness from the old barky flavours. The cover of

the bottle featured a colourful witch, in a Rosie the Riveter pose, biceps bulging, wand in hand, a skew-whiff patched and floppy witch's hat touching the top of the label, engulfed by swirls of emerald smoke.

3. Old old old – we called it 'Grapus', another way of saying goblin – one that is just the tiniest 5ml portion of a 1973 for each attendee. It is surprisingly pleasant, it is rich, but perhaps the flavours derive from the fact that it is a wonder to hold something in a glass crafted so long ago and imagine those who had a hand in its creation. Naturally, there was a goblin on the front, but depicted as a sort of Disney princess hybrid – long flowing hair intertwining with a long flowing beard, large doe eyes with lengthy lashes, and a finger up to their lips. Coquettish and grotesque.

The reactions to each one had been delicious – exactly what I had hoped for – shock and disgust giving way to delight at these new, weird ways of conveying the allure of their contents.

The absence of Susan was the only thing that tarnished these creations. She was so instrumental in my early development in the industry, and had assumed she would be a part of initial blending. I can't say exactly how I view her – mother figure, mentor, friend? But I had assumed too that she would be coming to stay with us at least a couple of times, and would be an integral part of our journey. Except she is too astute – she would know I was hiding something. By ignoring and even rebuffing her requests to visit, I had already aroused a suspicion in her – yet I knew I could not risk her coming at all because I could barely hold it together via flimsy texts. I could only imagine how easily I'd fold if she were in front of me in person. Her absence hurt, but her presence would harm us more.

However, my new crew were there as well as Donald and Rob – Linksy, Sheena and Bunty, all of whom had been giving a helping hand in all kinds of ways, from being sounding boards for our creative ideas to painting the outside of the completed buildings in a vast array of colours. It was them who helped me design and name our first batch of bottles. Despite all of them being older than me, and older than the intended market we wished to hit, they were so enthusiastic and seemed to know much more about whisky and marketing and even social media than I ever would have assumed. Bunty even corrected me when I made absurd generalisations about the over-sixties not having Facebook or not knowing how to use computers. Quite strongly, in fact.

I knew them well enough by then that their expressions and quirks of mouth and movements had been revealed to me. No matter how much we appeared to get on, each twitch or tug one way or the other added to my suspicions. Why had they chosen to spend so much of their time here? What was it that motivated them, kept them coming back?

I still hadn't ruled out Donald's connection to the bodies, but I was growing more certain that a woman had something to do with it. If not his father, what about his mother? What about this Julia woman? She continued working at the distillery till it closed in the eighties, but then, I supposed, so had everyone else.

The love and space in these people's hearts for whisky and this town was unparalleled – even someone like Bunty who didn't become part of the fabric of the town till she was much older. It was strange to think that at the time I was beginning my whisky journey, she was just making the transition to Campbeltown.

I didn't know how many more big transitions in life were ahead of me, but I hoped they would all contain Morag, that they would bring us closer instead of further away from each other. But then I remembered that I'd nearly messed it all up – and for what?

We'd fallen into a pattern or rhythm of some kind in our increased time spent together. I wasn't sure if it was worse than when we weren't speaking because at least then we were so far apart that change for the better was still a hope, but this . . . this pretending we were back to normal when we were anything but.

I was broken from my sad musings by an 'Och, Janet, get yer tit oot the gravy!'

I looked over to see the aforementioned Janet pulling back from reaching over the table for more potatoes. The sight of her with a large splodge of thick brown gravy dripping from her substantial chest was too much. I snorted so hard I had to excuse myself to check in a mirror whether the contents of my nose had expelled themselves in force onto my own chest.

By the time I came back, Linksy had the floor.

'I was saying on the course just this morn . . . mind you, January was a mite too early to start the golf season, I'll admit that now my fingers have regained some warmth, and this whisky is helping a lot, I'll tell you, and the ground was too hard–'

Someone cleared their throat loudly, and he paused to return to his point.

'Aye, really, I just wanted to say, I can't believe what you girls have done in such a short space of time. It's a dream come true. I thought I'd be brown bread long before I saw this distillery come back to life. In fact, I think us old ones can all agree, we never thought it'd happen. Not saying I'll stop drinking my Glen Scotia or Springbank, but this place has a special place in my heart. It was always a time for reflection, the wee walk from town to here, like how I feel on the green, except this twenty minutes or so is the perfect amount of time to think but not so long as to get to the dark thoughts. Morag, I think you wanted to say something?'

Morag never wants to speak to a crowd, despite the forced debates of her private education and how engagingly she addresses an audience.

She did that thing she was taught to do – hands firmly on hips and a wide solid stance. I know it grounds her, gives her confidence, but it does look a little unnatural. I never outwardly made fun of her for it, but it did always remind me of that episode of *Blackadder* where the actoorrrs teach Prince George how to give a speech.

Morag was wearing her old dependable green velvet trousers, which have stretched with her over the years. Usually, they pleasantly bulged at the hips, but they were sagging. How had I not noticed she'd lost so much weight?

As I looked at Morag, I thought how I'd never really considered myself a very sexual person till I met her. I was merely going through the motions based on what I thought I was supposed to do and feel and sound like based on what I'd seen on the telly or read in books or heard other girls discussing.

But when I met Morag, something changed. My hips were magnets to hers.

I shook myself a little as Morag began.

'Thank you to everyone gathered here today . . .' She laughed nervously and swayed, grabbing the edge of the table for support. 'Oh god, I sound like a wedding celebrant!

Her hands went back to her hips and she continued. 'But really – it's through your collective support and your being such cheerleaders and founts of knowledge that this has been possible. We still have a long way to go – as you know, we've only just put in our first batch of barley in the floors downstairs and some buildings are . . . unfinished, let's say.'

A few laughs and mutterings and glass clinkings interrupted her flow, but she smiled and waited before continuing. Her hands had reverted to holding the table.

'But here, today, our first bottlings, blended and made from the barrels still remaining, created by our predecessors, are done and in our hands and in our bellies. We hope we can do them proud and continue in the traditions of Ardkerran. I believe now we can really say that Ardkerran is a working distillery again.'

She stopped, narrowed her eyes, peered into the corner.

Many of us turned to glance the same way, to see what she was looking at, but there was nothing there. She shook her head and placed both hands on her hips again.

'I'd like to specifically welcome some of our patrons here, some of whom have flown all the way from America and Canada to be here. And battled through snow and crazy diversions due to fallen trees and landslides. Welcome to Scotland!'

I thought about what this distillery might mean to folk here. I had begun to realise that perhaps Morag and I had been a bit flippant in our purchasing of this place. We'd thought only about ourselves and how we might benefit from its renovation, and we had some lofty ideas about changing the face of whisky. I had become more fixated on the mystery of the bodies than on the distillery itself. Now I asked myself, did the bodies even matter?

To someone, somewhere, sometime or place perhaps. As it was, we had a responsibility now, to not only uphold what we had promised with Ardkerran, making something queer- and women-friendly, but to this community and its diaspora. Despite Morag being the more introverted of us two, I'd happily taken to the quieter life. Well, sort of; maybe it was just that I'd been glad to make my own missions and purpose here.

As the night went on, everyone switching seats inter-mittently to engage in new conversations, Morag and I moved closer and closer to each other.

We ended up in a riotous conversation with a couple of the tourists from far away, during which we were even finishing each other's sentences and patting arms and pouring each other drinks. I raised my hopes that she might, for the first night in a long time, come and sleep in the same bed as me.

But she didn't. As if startled by something, she left early, and swiftly, without looking back at me at all.

CHAPTER 27

Morag
2024

No matter where I went, I couldn't escape them. The ghosts of Alistair and Duncan.

Sometimes it was just a hand, a severed, chewed-up hand, inching towards me or appearing over my shoulder. Once, I woke up convinced it had been holding my mouth closed, blocking my nose, squeezing my cheeks together in a death grip while I slept.

I couldn't sleep much, after that.

I kept turning over my to-do list in my mind. I had taken to wandering round the distillery grounds with no torch, no lights on. Then I started going for drives at night.

There wasn't one drive I could do without a fierce wind buffeting the car, and more than once I thought the firm, muscular arms of the men were pushing with all their might into the sides of the little vehicle. That they were intent on tipping me over or else forcing me into the ditch. Or into the sea.

Sometimes I let go of the steering wheel. Just for a moment.

Right then I was waiting at the beach at the tip of the peninsula, staring over into the limitless sea. I'd spent the last three hours driving round and round the same loop: Campbeltown, South End, Machrihanish, Campbeltown, South End, Machrihanish . . .

I wailed the whole way.

I let myself. I knew if I didn't, I'd do something awful.

I don't cry – it's something my friends always poked fun at me for. Even at my best friend's wedding, I forced it, just so she could have the joy of saying that she was the one who made me, who could break my hard heart. Eilidh cries at anything. Even the opening bars of 'My Heart Will Go On' by Celine Dion. Although, to be fair, that's usually only once she's finished watching *Titanic* for the umpteenth time.

I know it wasn't fair on her. I wasn't being fair on her. I couldn't hold myself together in front of her. I couldn't explain myself to her. I could only snap or say nothing right now. Sometimes I could pretend; when other people were around, I had to. But the ghosts were appearing with increasing frequency, and increasing solidity.

As I wailed, the ghosts wailed with me.

At least, I think they were ghosts. They seemed pretty solid. They both put on their seatbelts when I told them to.

I'd been keeping track of Eilidh's browser history. She'd probably forgotten that I knew her password. Maybe she thought I wouldn't look. Her laptop password was my name. I saw the article she had bookmarked, of the two men. Our two men. Alistair and Duncan.

I addressed them that way from then on, when I saw them.

I even asked them questions sometimes. Like they were pets or babies I was carting around. They couldn't speak, though. When they opened their mouths there was no tongue. Just whisky-sodden sawdust.

But they could still wail.

I'd made myself a camp in the office. It became my den. My 'insomnia den', I'd called it when I spoke to Eilidh. She knew I'd made these before, during my previous bouts of sleeplessness.

Her first experience of it was during the pandemic. I hadn't had an episode since we started dating. She was so soothing. Or maybe distracting. It used to frustrate her, for a period, when I demanded she come to bed at the same time as me, or that time we had one of our rare screaming arguments because she stayed out drinking till four, knowing I had my Edinburgh half-marathon the next day and I needed her beside me to sleep.

Maybe I was unreasonable.

She should try living with her. The amount of chargers, headphones and assorted other things I've had to replace because they disappeared into the ether with her. My good pens!

Ten years. We've been together ten years. Maybe this is our end. Maybe this is what would break us.

I didn't think I'd said anything aloud, but Duncan and

Alistair both nodded slowly and deeply at me.

It was the most time I'd ever spent in the company of men. Men and no other women, anyway. Most of my friends were lesbians or lesbian adjacent. It was easier that way.

Eilidh didn't understand what it's like for older lesbians. And I'm not even that old.

Although I thought forty was old, once.

Was this the end?

Was this our end?

Maybe, they nodded again.

The distillery was nowhere near being completed. We could celebrate the small wins, for sure, like the injunction being killed and our first whiskies going out into the world

But Eilidh had changed. Maybe no one should be together this long. Maybe marriage is a sham. Maybe once the life expectancy of human beings extended and we started living beyond thirty we should have embraced something else.

Maybe I did want to be a mother and now I'd missed my chance.

Maybe I should have done a PhD instead of whatever we were doing all those years in Edinburgh.

Maybe my life would be better. Maybe her life would be better.

Maybe life would be better without me in it.

Duncan didn't move. But Alistair shook his head.

I sighed and stepped out of the car. I was so sick of the wind but I couldn't deny that it helped me breathe again.

Right.

Right.

Right.

Come on, I told myself. Can't mope for ever.

Big girl pants on?

Big girl pants on.

What a ridiculous expression.

I tried a few others to get me going, to cut my brain's spiralling.

What's for you won't go by you.

Whit's for ye willnae go by ye.

This too shall pass.

Every breath is a new beginning.

Willnae.

Won't.

Wouldn't.

Eilidh wouldn't listen. She'd always done her own thing. Said she couldn't help herself.

We should have been celebrating. Together. But I wasn't. She was overjoyed at the mounds of barley she'd secured and god knows what else, but I knew they were just the beginning. Why the fuck do they insist a whisky has to sit in barrels for three years to earn the right to call itself Scotch whisky? It's only a year or two in America. We had barely made it this far, and I didn't have a plan anymore. I didn't have anything to tether me.

God knows what those great big mash tuns will look like after last night's rain.

Did she cover them? Did I cover them?

Did I get in one? I think I did. I think I wished for the wooden lid to cover me in darkness and for the blades of the rotating arm to slice me into bits.

CHAPTER 28

Eilidh

2024

I woke up and needed Morag. Or maybe she needed me. I can't explain why, but I felt it intensely. I turned on the torch on my phone and took Bruno with me.

It had snowed, and everything seemed muffled and formless. I don't think I even put shoes on and I definitely hadn't remembered to pull my trusty beanie on over my ears.

She wasn't in the office where she'd been sleeping all these weeks. The wee heater was on, blazing and noisy, her blankets were in a pile on the floor and her phone was on the desk.

I kept talking out loud to Bruno, and he seemed to understand we were on a mission. He seemed to tell me he was with me, wherever I had to go.

The car wasn't in its usual spot. I could see tyre tracks leading out of the distillery gates, which were half open, and my heart shuddered.

That's when I heard the wailing. It sounded like a gang of poltergeists had gathered to sing at the end of the world.

It wasn't like anything I had ever heard before. We followed the apocalyptic sound, and in my mind I pretended I was Velma or someone brave from *Scooby Doo*. I wasn't frightened. I wasn't. Bruno's ear was pressed as flat as I had ever seen it.

As we got closer, the sounds became sharper, and I realised it was Morag. Crying.

There was a ladder against one of the mash tuns.

I tied Bruno to a pipe. He was so shivery, from cold or fear, I couldn't be sure, but I didn't think he'd run away. He was with me till the end.

I climbed up and aimed my phone light over the top. Morag didn't stop crying; she just took her arms away from her face and peered up, shielding her eyes from the glare.

I placed my phone under my arm and attempted to jump down, hanging onto the side one-handed. She leaped straight into my arms and shoved her face into me, still howling, knee deep in water.

It didn't take long for her to gulp and splutter and stop. She looked up at me and kissed me.

It was wet and snotty, but I was ecstatic.

I felt in control, the more grown up of the two of us for once, as I led all three of us back to the caravan and towelled us all down in turn. Morag sat like a sad little kid who had been made to get out of the pool early. Bruno had three blankets around him, just his intermittently sighing snout sticking out.

Morag and I swayed and cuddled and laughed and rubbed each other's arms and shoulders warm.

'Eilidh.'

'Yes?' When she didn't speak, I squeezed her knee gently. She took a deep breath before bursting out into hysterical laughter.

'I think I just had a breakdown.'

I started laughing too, and we somehow communicated so much more than we had in months in wheezed half-words between fits of laughter.

'That isn't funny, Morag. That's actually very serious.'

But we didn't stop for an age, till we collapsed backwards onto the bed, our legs and arms slotting right into place around each other, like two well-cut puzzle pieces, like we had since the beginning. I wiped the tears from her face and pushed her damp hair back from her forehead.

'I'm still mad at you, Eilidh.'

All I could say over and over again was, 'I know, I know.'

We stayed up till the light started filtering between the ragged caravan curtain. Bruno had managed to push himself further and further into us so we were left with a mere slip of bed, but that was okay with us.

She told me about what had been happening with her all those weeks when I'd been so wrapped up in my own melancholy. I wanted to go slowly and gently with her, let her lead the conversation; I knew she would need some real help soon, but I didn't want to suggest anything yet. Her driving at all hours – how hadn't I noticed? Her seeing the ghosts, seeing Duncan and Alistair. Her knowing exactly what I had been up to this whole time. Well, she didn't mention Donald, so I could only hope that piece of news never, ever reached her.

What had I done? I'd thought she'd seemed a bit off, but I'd interpreted it as her being off with me, which I suppose it was, but it was far, far more than that. She had lost herself, she said.

'Are we a bit too co-dependent?' Morag finally said.

'I don't think there's such a thing.'

Bruno seemed to snort in agreement. Or perhaps it was a 'How do you think I feel next to you two?' derisive kind of snort. I couldn't tell.

'I'm sorry, I really am.' I tried to explain myself, but I didn't want to say anything that would risk our refound closeness. 'I completely, well, totally disregarded your feelings. I didn't realise . . . I didn't understand that you were so affected by the, um, what do you want me to refer them as?'

'Dead bodies is fine. Or shall we have a codename? Like . . . I can't think of anything witty.'

I searched my usually fizzing-with-ideas brain, but I couldn't either. 'Dead bodies then, but we can sleep on it, when we eventually do sleep that is. I'm sorry – I still see them as something intriguing. Even now we know their names.'

She propped herself up on her elbow at that. 'Go on,' she said. 'Tell me what you've discovered about them. Even though I made it clear I wanted to keep them out of sight and mind, and that's what you should have borne in mind, no matter how much I told you about how I really felt about them. I mean–'

'No, it's fine, you're right.'

Morag lay back down again, pulled her glasses off and passed them to me to place on the side. I just stared for a while before answering her. I really badly wanted to smell her neck, but I held myself back. I didn't want to get my hopes up again.

'Alistair and Duncan both worked here at the distillery,' I began. 'They were two of the blenders or distillers or something, I'm not quite sure. But the newspaper report said they drowned in the loch.'

'I did wonder about that. I did read it, but I wasn't sure what to make of it.'

'Yeah, exactly. But there can't have been any bodies – the ones we have are *definitely* these two chaps. They worked with Donald's dad too – Hugh. I think . . . I think they were lovers. Duncan and Alistair, not Hugh. The love letters Sheena found might be from one of them. God knows why they kept them there, though. I mean, here, at the distillery.

'All I could find out about them was that they were both born and bred here – and they owned a boat together. There was wee snippet in the *Courier* about them being drunk and disorderly one night, maybe a year before their supposed "drowning". They were mucking about on the water and needed to be rescued. Their boat was found adrift after their disappearance and nothing more was done to find them – it was just assumed they drowned after a night out. They were in their thirties, I think, if I remember correctly.'

'Fascinating. And why those awful tartan suits?'

'Oh, fuck knows!'

We were quiet for a while, and I could tell Morag's

breath was deepening. I couldn't let her go to sleep yet though.

'Morag, what do you need? To feel good? To feel better? To feel safe?'

'Mmmhmm . . . I need . . . I need neither of us to ever talk about those men again after this. To know you're not researching them. For the foreseeable. And a project. A purpose. A plan.'

By the time I went to reply, she was already asleep.

CHAPTER 29

Eilidh
2024

I had become obsessed with Julia Murray.

She'd wormed her way into my dreams, however absurd or sinister or mundane they were. One nightmare involved being asked to sing on stage – she was a judge, on a bizarre island with Bruno as a talking jellyfish who was somehow racing me – she was there, with a stopwatch; after one where I was trying to explain why Xander was the weakest character in *Buffy* and she was a bartender serving drinks, the ice clinking in the cocktail shaker in the dreamworld being replaced by the click-clacking of the branches along the caravan window, I woke up feeling as if I had fallen ten feet. Always with long red hair and in a tartan skirt and blazer.

I still hadn't excluded Donald's dad, Hugh, and maybe I was naive, too trusting, but if he'd raised Donald – or so I reasoned – I couldn't see how he could have done it. I had at least ruled out Donald protecting the family secret at any cost, but the nagging doubt lingered. I've always been too easily manipulated. I assume good intentions. Donald could have been leading me into a false sense of security all this time. Maybe we weren't really friends.

My initial hunch, when we first revealed the pale skin of the men in the barrels, was that a man had murdered them. Why wouldn't I have assumed that? It follows that only a man could overpower two other men who, according to my inexperienced eyes, appeared to have been murdered in the same incident. Also, I'm aware that most murders and violent crimes are committed by men.

But why couldn't women murder too? The truth is they do. The truth is they are plenty strong enough. Didn't Morag pride herself in being able to do more push-ups than the average man? Still, I couldn't work out motive – the only sensible one seemed to be that the two men had tried to hurt her somehow.

I couldn't accept that the murderer wouldn't be found. I needed closure. I needed this to end. I couldn't move on unless it did.

Morag had been very clear – for her to feel safe, I had to stop looking.

But I couldn't. Even knowing the cost if she found out. Even remembering a splinter of the feeling I had when we were apart.

The internet was next to useless – even with me now using incognito tabs and deleting as much as I could – and the only thing I could find out was all the planning permission requests made to Argyll and Bute Council during the last fifty years.

There was one Murray – just one. A Mrs F. Murray. They had requested something daft like a more modern replacement for a crumbling stone dyke that defied upkeep yet had been protected under some arcane law.

I stared and stared at the map, the red outline of the property. It wasn't far from here. Could I get up and go without Morag noticing?

She had been more watchful than usual. That was to be expected. I should have been more hurt that she was expecting me to break her trust, except, well, I was.

The sun was out, glaring across my laptop screen, even through the mucky windows of Aladdin's Cave, as we have decided to name it officially, capital letters and everything. It's been my hideout. I adore being surrounded by mess. Most people don't understand.

It was probably the first sign something was 'wrong' with me, when I really thought about it. Labelled as lazy and careless and gross, but, really, I liked the disorder. I spoil anything clean and orderly, so it's much less stressful on my mind if I am in and about clutter. No matter what I do, what I accidentally spill or forget about, I can't make the space worse. I can't ruin anything. And having things out, and in piles – it is the system computers use, after all – most recently accessed sits on top, in the cache. Invariably when I put something somewhere 'safe' that means it's gone from my mind and I can't find it again, so I tend to leave things out.

I found one of the sturdier buckets to stand on, to see if I could spy on Morag from there.

She was co-ordinating the painting and decorating of our newly finished events space.

It was our joint idea: Morag needs continual projects, and the distillation of whisky was really best left to the people we had hired. This way, with the space, we could give back to the community – offer a free space for groups to meet, for local people to perform, for visitors to host their clan meetings when the Scottish diaspora from Canada, America, Australia and beyond arrive to this remote corner of Scotland. I love their vision of us. They get to experience and see Scotland as this centre of Celtic culture, and the people who live here get to be reminded of Scotland's power and beauty, beyond the humdrum of everyday reality. It is because of them we breathe in the hills again, rather than just letting them exist as part of the background. We also had fun mixing up our ideas of Celtic culture; we thought we might host a drag king night or open mics, maybe poetry evenings.

But as for now, Morag would definitely know if I took the car – not least because it had started emitting horrific screeches whenever we started it, noises that continued for the first mile or two till the engine was warmed up.

So I told her I was visiting Bunty – that she had found some old books of her father's that she wanted to pass on. The truth was, I didn't even know where she lived and she'd never given me her number. Morag didn't question me, but perhaps her eyes lingered too long on mine.

With the destination typed into my maps, I set off for the old farmer's cottage with the stone dyke that was never approved to be destroyed, with no idea who lived there now, or whether the Mrs F. Murray who made the request was even linked to Julia Murray, or whether Julia Murray even had anything at all to do with Alistair and Duncan. But it was a clue, a direction to head in, and a better one than the Freemasons, which thus far had turned up nothing except the fact that a surprising amount of people were members. Which didn't help narrow anything down for me.

It was a beautiful drive. It reassured me – how could I be doing something wrong if everything around me told me this was meant to be? Every little bleat from the sheep, each waving shaft of barley, all the birds swooping and swirling in a pattern created only for me – all these things just made me surer of myself.

My maps, of course, did not take me quite the right route, and I ended up traversing one of the most potholed tracks I ever had the misfortune to drive along, which is saying something given that I had been across so many of Scotland's remote islands and rural villages in my time. I patted the wee car's dashboard and thanked her for all her miles so far and reassured her we'd get through this too.

When I at last reached my destination, there was no obvious place to park, so I smushed the car onto a muddy verge and hoped I would be able to rev her back out again.

Smoke puttered from the long slim chimney pipe with its conical hat. Ivy and roses wound their way tenaciously across the walls of the one-storey house, ending in a thicket twisted with brambles, like the base of a lavish and gothic wedding dress. Beside an upturned wheelbarrow, a ginger cat licked its paws and feigned nonchalance while eyeing a pair of woodpigeons cooing nearby. And I could see a woman sitting by the window, holding a large mug in stiff, wrinkled hands.

I took in her large green cardigan.

Her brilliant white perm.

Her very familiar perfectly round glasses.

It was Bunty.

I cross-checked the image of the map from the planning permission records with the map on my phone – I was definitely in the right place.

I'd ended up at Bunty's after all.

And that's when she noticed me – as the cat lunged for the pigeons and snaffled one in its sharp claws. The second pigeon flapped off into the sky with a screech that could rival the car's cold engine.

I raised one hand no higher than my shoulder as if to wave hello. I couldn't work out the expression on her face when she mirrored me with her hand. I don't know how long we waited like that, before she turned her hand around and gestured me in.

Bunty's house smelled exactly how I expected it to – the warmth of oats undercut by the mustiness of old books and trinkets. The kitchen was the back corner of her living room, and she wittered away as she clanked and clattered about, making me a tea. She came over with some homemade shortbread just as I was testing the springiness of the burnt red armchair I was in. It had those old creaky metal springs, masked by three layers of cushions flattened by decades of use.

What should I ask her? How should I explain how I ended up here?

'Lovely wee place here, Bunty,' was all I could manage, but I wasn't sure whether my tone came across as genuine.

'Aye, thank you, hen. I found this place when I came here, oh, when was it, a decade or so ago now.'

'Why? I mean, why Campbeltown? If you . . . if you're not from here, what drew you here? Where does your family come from?'

'Och, I can't really explain. I guess you could say I was looking for . . . for home. Something away from it all. Something near the sea. I didn't fancy an island – too beholden to the ferries. As you know, I do like a dram here and there, and I wondered what Campbeltown had to offer, since it's a whisky region all of its own. As for my family, they're not around anymore. Nothing to tie me anywhere.'

'What's your real name?'

She spluttered her tea at that. 'What do you mean?'

'Well, Bunty is usually a nickname or a pet name, I think. Is it instead of Elizabeth?'

'Aye, um, Elizabeth Murphy. That's me.'

'Murphy. That's weird,' I mused as I dunked a slice of shortbread in my tea.

'Why is that weird?'

'Uh, I don't know.'

'What did you come for anyway?' She looked at me sharply. 'Did Sheena tell you where I stay?'

Shit. What was a plausible reason? I knew if I told her Sheena told me, she would certainly bring it up with Sheena, at least as something worth mentioning, and then Sheena would say that she didn't.

'Oh, a weird coincidence really,' I said as confidently as I could. 'I was . . . I was looking for . . . There was a local farmer who had said something about possibly using one of his fields for barley for us. But my maps–' That felt like a good path to follow and I clung to it for dear life. 'Yeah, my maps took me the wrong way so I decided to park up. That's when . . . when I noticed you. Thought I'd say hi.'

'Oh, which farmer?' she asked, snapping a chunk of shortbread in half. 'I can direct you. Do you have their number? I've got the number of a few round here in my address book – in case I need to let them know of any escaping sheep, haha.'

'Don't worry about it, I'll sort it out later.'

I smiled, hopefully in a reassuring way, and scanned the room for something to comment on, to divert the increasingly uncomfortable conversation, and that's when my eyes landed on the pictures over the mantelpiece. A family with red hair: a mum, dad, two boys and a girl . . .

Bunty went to get up, saying, 'Are you sure? It's no bother. Wait a minute–'

'No! I mean, no, please don't worry yourself.'

'Och, no need to worry about bothering an old lady. Here, give me a hand.'

It was a bit of a struggle to get up out of that old chair

myself, but I hauled Bunty to her feet and then walked swiftly to the door.

'Right, I best be off now,' I said as airily as possible, before doing the fastest walk I could manage without breaking into a jog. I slammed the car door shut and took off without putting my seatbelt on, not daring to look back towards the house.

★

As soon as I got home, I paid the exorbitant fee required to access census records, birth and marriage certificates on a heritage website. The woman who lived in the stone dyke house before had two sons and a daughter. The daughter's name: Julia Evelyn Murray.

Was it too much of a leap to conclude that was the same woman, the same family, who now sat on Bunty's fireplace?

Bunty said herself she hadn't come here till a few years ago . . . but what if she was simply returning home?

CHAPTER 30

You
2024

It feels like time has stopped. You've enjoyed the quiet life, tried to keep busy, tried to appreciate your new friends, your peace.

But now you're spending more time around the distillery, now the sweet smell of whisky brewing has returned, your mind increasingly wanders again and again to them. To Alistair and Duncan.

Maybe you did love them. They were certainly the first people to show you another way of living, to share your voracious need to know more, to care about the details.

That's why the betrayal hurt so much, why you lashed out. That's what you reassure yourself.

You should have noticed the signs – it was more gradual than you had supposed at the time. They had begun to pull away from you, to be more secretive. Duncan especially had started quoting all sorts of whisky barons and capitalists, but you thought your shared love of Voltaire would trump all that. You thought he was playing devil's advocate. Not that he had become the devil itself.

CHAPTER 31

Eilidh

2024

'Are you sure?'

'Absolutely! Mind out, though, if you have any holes in your shoes, you will definitely go home with barley in them, and it gets *everywhere*. It's like glitter – you'll be cleaning it up for weeks.'

Heather looked at me like it was unthinkable she'd have holes in her shoes, but I could see Zahir and Gordon pulling up theirs to check. Gordon tugged at the front of his left boot where the upper had started to pull away from the base.

We were walking into the room above the kiln where barley was piled inches high and held aloft above the kiln by netting.

'Isn't it, um, against health and safety or something to have our dirty shoes in the barley?' Zahir asked as he adjusted the brightness of a light he was carrying.

I reassured them that I had done this on multiple whisky distillery tours before, or ones where they dried their barley for their whisky in-house, anyway.

'Cor, you could take a cosy wee nap in here,' marvelled Gordon.

'It does smell incredible,' Heather agreed. 'Like those heat-up microwaveable animals you get.'

We stayed there long enough for Heather to decide it was too dark to get any decent shots, before we gingerly made our way down the thin metal ladder one at a time, everyone passing heavy camera equipment along between them.

We'd already walked through the malting floor, picked up the grains in our hand and examined the little shoots starting to emerge. I'd encouraged them to eat them too – pleasantly fluffy and squashy. We'd looked into the deep bath where the barley was steeped before being spread out on the floor, and Gordon had even, almost absentmindedly, trailed his hands to and fro in figures of eight, humming a gentle tune I couldn't quite place.

'Only a handful of distilleries undertake every single part of the process. I wanted us to be one of those – I wanted not only to say I, or we, the team, have control over every part of the process, but I am a nosy, curious kind of person and I want to eventually experiment as much as possible with each stage. Like, what if we added something to the water we steep the barley in? Would that affect the germination process? Or even the final flavour? Plus, it is what Ardkerran did before. We want to continue that, and it would be a waste not to use every bit of this distillery we are now custodians of.'

I was trying to interpret Heather's stoic face again and,

as I often do, I added my own most negative thoughts onto that face's blank canvas. She thinks I'm pretentious, talking rubbish, acting like I know more than I do. I shook my head and reminded myself that maybe, just maybe, she wasn't thinking those things.

'Remind us, why do you need to add barley to water? Is it just to dry it out again?'

'Well—'

'And add the question into your answer. Please. I'm editing myself out of this, remember?'

'Ah, yes. Well, um, we need to add barley to water to steep to essentially trick it into starting to germinate. What we want to capture are the sugars that it begins to convert from its starch. Look at this one.' I always had bits of barley in my pockets somehow. 'Pull it apart and see the fluffy insides.'

Zahir got me to repeat this process several times under different lights. I could sense that my excitement was fading somewhat with the repetitiveness needed for filming.

'Then it gets turned over on the floor several times over days. We control the temperatures in a very technical way – we open and close windows accordingly, haha!'

No one else laughed.

'Right. Then what?'

'After that, we place the barley, now sometimes referred to as "green malt" into the bit we just came from – uh – into the netting above the kiln. We add peat to the kiln, which imparts a delicious smoky flavour to the barley. Typically, a heavy peated whisky would be about forty parts per million with a maximum of about fifty parts. And when I say parts, I mean *phenol parts per million*, phenols being the chemicals that attach themselves to the malt and give us that smoky taste I mentioned before. We are aiming a bit below that for our first batches – we really want to hit a happy medium initially and not have it be the central character; we want to see what we can experiment with in every stage that affects the final flavour. Check out Bruichladdich, though; Jim McEwan really wanted to see how far he could take peat and they have one called Octomore which is, I can't remember the exact number, but it's over one hundred and fifty parts!'

That got a reaction, at least.

'And what does that taste like?'

I made a face at Zahir's question. 'It's an experience – I wouldn't drink it on most occasions, but it's undeniable what McEwan has done for the industry, and now we know where our limits are, where the edge is. It goes really well with an odourful cheese known as "Minger", let's just say that.'

I paused and waited to see what they wanted next. I could feel my attention slipping and wondered if it was time to take my meds yet. I should have brought a snack with me.

I lovingly stroked our grinder, a rare specimen from years ago, and explained that we had to alter the level we set it to depending on the type of barley. Although coarse barley is sometimes more readily available in this region, the mill did not do well with it.

I was hesitant to lead them to our new mash tuns.

Seeing Morag crying in a collapsed heap – the antithesis of her solid, assured self – was still raw. She had refused any help so far, claiming she was fine, and I had been trying really hard not to appraise her with a pitying head-tilt, but I was concerned.

We reached them anyway, and they were in full force, churning and frothing and making quite a din. Zahir kept shaking his head every time I started a sentence – he couldn't pick me up clearly over the noise, so I started shouting.

'The grist, the powder we get after milling, is mixed with hot water in the mash tuns. We source our water from the same place the other distilleries do. Nothing like Scottish spring water, eh? What we have after is called "wort", a sweet sugary liquid. Then the yeast. And that's one of the reasons I love whisky – it is just three ingredients: barley, water, yeast. It is a craft. No two people would make the same whisky from it. Some people say it is better than an oral history, that making whisky is a *flavour* history. We're tasting a drink that has been made here for hundreds of years, using very similar processes. We're standing here, discussing the same decisions, the same elements, as people have done since they first brewed it at home.'

Heather nodded once at that – which I took as a sign that she absolutely loved it.

'Oh, and I forgot to say, we cool the wort before we add the yeast. This is where fermentation commences – the yeast feeds on the sugars and that's what makes the alcohol. Look at this one.'

I opened the porthole in the top of the furthermost mash

tun. Inside it was frothing violently. It felt like me. Despite that, despite how I was feeling, walking them through the process of making whisky was weirdly soothing. I was on familiar ground. I was reciting the stages I had heard and written about so many times before.

And this was mine.

We reached the two gleaming copper stills in the next room, both so tall they reached into the room below. Atlas was there, staring, rubbing their hat vigorously over their hair, clearly puzzling over something. I tapped them on the shoulder and they jumped up comically, and I could just imagine a big exclamation mark appearing over their head, as if they were a character in a game I had interacted with.

'Hi, Atlas. How goes it?'

'Hmm, I'm not sure. I think, yes, and then . . .'

'Would you be able to explain this part of the process to the BBC team?'

'Hmm, oh, yes, of course – see the necks? These ones taper in such a way that we think – well, we hope – hmm, well, I *know* should produce something a little sweeter. It sort of vaporises and then we get it to go through into the worm – the copper coil I made is immersed in cold running water and then we turn the vapour into a liquid again. There's a residue called pot ale – that's what we're collecting to be used in thingy's skincare thingy . . .'

They trailed off and started rubbing their hat again. I gave Atlas a wee smile and thumbs-up, which they happily returned, and I motioned for the others to move on and let Atlas get on with whatever they were working on.

I took Heather, Gordon and Zahir along to the spirit safe.

'Only the pure centre cut, also known as the heart, is collected in the spirit receiver. Everything else goes round and round again. We're aiming for sixty-eight per cent alcohol by volume. Do you want to try some?'

The reactions were mixed to say the least: Gordon lapped the tip of his tongue in and out, like a cat; Zahir took one deep huff and then pushed the glass as far away from his face as possible; Heather downed hers in one gulp and let out a hot hard flash of breath.

'I would compare it to firewater or moonshine, if you've ever had such a thing. Homebrewed spirits, essentially. It's strong and clear.'

Zahir coughed. 'Why so strong?'

'Well, over the years of maturation in a cask, we lose a lot of the liquid. It's called–'

'The angel's share,' Gordon finished for me.

'Yes, that's right. But before that, it's this. This is good and sweet.'

Zahir didn't look like he believed that part.

I smiled to myself and continued my tour. 'This is where you know whether you have a good product on your hands. If the new make, this stuff, is poor, then no further steps can save it. Now to my favourite bit. The casks. Even if you have a superb new make, the maturation can ruin it. They say a bad cask is like a bad marriage . . .'

I paused while I considered this phrase that was oft-repeated in the whisky industry – what kind of cask did Morag and I have? Perhaps we could do a second maturation, move our relationship, our spirit, to something new, to create a better finish.

I took them into the next building, where we had around fifty new barrels, standing, waiting for their purpose. Some of these would, hopefully, be at the distillery for years to come.

'Here are the casks we have bought in from Europe. Sherry, mostly. It gives the final drink a redder tinge, as you'd expect, but also adds flavours. What goes in is clear, and what comes out is something amber, something reddish, something yellow brown. What goes in is a strong booze, with a handful of notes, but they can be hard to parse through that intense, cutting alcohol. What comes out is something layered, something balanced, something that can be savoured and enjoyed.'

We waited as Gordon and Zahir filmed the casks from different angles, murmuring between themselves as they set up each shot.

Heather was not one for small talk, I had learned by then. So, although silences scare me, I waited in silence.

Finally, the moment I had been dreading.

The warehouse.

Again, we had to wait for the two guys, this time as they set up just the right configuration of lights in order to film in the cavernous place.

'Tell us about the fire,' Heather prompted once the camera was pointed at me.

'It happened . . .' I corrected myself. '*The fire* happened on Hogmanay. Right there in that corner. The police and the firefighters said it was started by a cigar. They chalked it up to someone, one of the revellers, enjoying a nighttime smoke, a way to see in the bells, perhaps. Thankfully, because it started from the outside and these walls are stone and damp, it only set fire to the roof. You can still see scorch marks, and I don't know if you can tell, but there's all kinds of ivy and suchlike growing in here – but the fire burned all the moss away there. Everything, aside from the roof and, haha, me, stayed intact. It was an accident.'

'That's it, that's all they had to say about it?'

I didn't want to touch that sore wound any further. If we hadn't been concealing such a grisly secret with the potential to ruin us, I would have been devastated at the lack of drive from the police. I couldn't believe it was an accident.

'Yep. I mean, yes. But, here, what about something else I can show you.' I drew them quickly away from that line of questioning with most people's favourite part of a whisky tour – drinking the stuff.

Zahir was much happier with this activity – sampling straight from the casks, something matured and amber, something a little less strong than the new make we had tried earlier. He said he felt lucky that this was his job.

But as we sampled, I noticed something strange. Something that linked up with the change in handwriting I had noticed in the distillery notebooks so many weeks before – the whisky was noticeably lovelier from around 1974 onwards. Three years after the murders, three years after these men were killed, the product was noticeably . . . smoother.

And, with that, the filming was over.

I waved them off, the last dram still in my hand, undrunk. I wouldn't miss them. Perhaps in another life, a life where I wasn't hiding something so monumental, I might have enjoyed it, might have enjoyed their company or tried to get to know them, tried to show them more nooks and crannies of the place. As it was, it felt like a tension pulling me in two directions – give them enough that the documentary shows us and all we've done in a good light, brings people to us, but not so much that they linger. The longer they stayed, the deeper they delved into our distillery, the more likely they would come across what we had tried to hide.

But they were gone, at last, and now I could focus on trying to win my wife back. I hadn't realised just how keenly I felt the worry and the weight of the filming. Not just because I wasn't sure we would ever complete this renovation or escape the feeling of being perceived so intensely, but because of the constant presence of the dead bodies, those heavy, malignant, oppressive things, which even now could still be revealed, could still cause us terrible harm.

They had already harmed us.

It was time for me to finish this once and for all. I needed to tie up all the loose ends. I knew who the men were. But who was Julia Murray?

CHAPTER 32

Eilidh
2024

Bunty. Julia. Bunty. Julia. I found lots of Elizabeth Murphys across the UK, but none born in Scotland at the right time. I suppose she could have been born elsewhere and then brought up here. Her accent *was* a bit strange, like Scots words and the rhotic r sounds and other European languages were placed into a dice cup, shaken, and the resulting blunted shapes poured onto the table were what her mouth moved around.

I'd never questioned how Bunty knew so much about whisky – she seemed, more than any of the others, to know the intricate steps of distilling. When we tasted together, she picked up my threads where I dropped them. She'd go off on rants and tangents that rivalled my own. I realised I'd never asked any of them what they did for a living. I was prejudiced. I'd assumed the older generation had not much left to give and forgotten one of my key tenets – that everyone has an interesting story to tell. What was Bunty's?

Without any more evidence, the only option I had now was to rule everyone else out.

Why not Sheena?

Why not Linksy?

Why not Rob?

Why not Donald's father, Hugh?

Why not someone else entirely?

But why not Bunty?

And so, to answer my own questions, I began inviting them all along to regular meetings, giving them any job I could find. They'd been so useful in our initial bottlings made from the whisky of the old barrels and now they could be a part of the new, a blending of ages and times and community, and I could keep them close.

Together, we discussed the future of Ardkerran and its place in Campbeltown, its place in Scottish whisky. I'll admit, it was useful having such life experience, such intimate knowledge of the area, in my hands.

Donald could offer what he knew about the foreign market from the tourists who had frequented his pub over the years: their preferred tastes, the narratives behind the whisky they most attached themselves to. Plus, how we could position ourselves on the shelves so that a customer might select us over any other of the whisky bottles.

Sheena took no prisoners. She was brutal but thoughtful in critiquing everything the rest of us said. Like me, she was relentless in putting forward the notion that women be considered the primary segment of our target market.

Linksy represented the old market – the men to whom

whisky was still sold, despite being so young when he began as a cooper's apprentice in the seventies. He gave us insight into the male mind and into what Scotland represented for him. Mostly, he told his exaggerated stories, but they are an ethnography in themselves.

Rob was similar but, if anything, he was more representative of that golden era of nostalgia. He was the man you see holding up the bar every day, who would walk to buy his daily newspaper, who genuinely knew what it was like to have a cold hard day at sea and what a panacea whisky is for such a day.

And Bunty . . . Bunty encouraged us to think globally, beyond even what Donald knew. She began opening up, telling us of her travels across the world and how she had found whisky there. When I presented a slide of images of potential customers, she clapped her hands together in front of her mouth and gave a squeak. Initially, I wasn't sure how to interpret it, but she qualified by saying: 'Yes, aye – all of this, all of them.'

Together, we shaped what the future of Ardkerran looked like, and it was weird and queer and neon.

I had begun to take notes of the places Bunty had been and the phrases she used, which pointed towards a deeper knowledge of whisky than I ever could have expected. I tallied it with the distillery records of Julia Murray and her couple of years as the ambassador for this place. Hokkaido in Japan, Kentucky in America, Cologne in Germany, Galicia in Spain. It all fitted.

I hoped I was subtle, that she couldn't read my

excitement swirled with dread, my side eyes in between my genuine expressions of joy at what we were creating together.

When I felt I had enough, I told them I would be taking a week off, to assimilate, to plan, to turn our mind maps and ideas into something concrete, a business plan or similar.

But, really, I was gearing up for days spent pulling together my new-found evidence.

CHAPTER 33

You

2024

It is inevitable now.

You will be found out.

Should you run or face the truth?

Maybe it is all in your head, but you sense that Eilidh definitely knows.

Alistair and Duncan have started following you around again. In the morning, on your daily walk into town to fetch the paper – something to get up and dressed for – they join you. At night, when you read your book, sometimes one of them turns the page for you. Throughout the day, they peer around corners, sit on the edges of bars and tables and beams, legs crossed and hands clasped, staring.

You start crafting your tale. What happened and when and why. You think it is all true – the bits you remember are true anyway. All the embellishments seem . . . plausible. Most likely.

You must tell it in such a way that you seem innocent. You must tell it in such a way that you believe you did the right thing, even though you aren't sure anymore.

All's well that ends well, and the distillery is looking better than it ever has. So is the whisky. That's all that matters. In the end, you did the right thing.

CHAPTER 34

Eilidh
2024

'I know who did it.'

Morag looked incredulous, and I couldn't blame her.

I looked insane.

My hair had been put up into a messy bun for so many days in a row without washing, I think the matted clumps were what was holding the last of my sanity together. For the previous three days, I had worn my pyjamas at night, then put my dungarees over the top, and then taken the dungarees off again to sleep. Without removing the pyjamas underneath. I did not change my socks and I did not wear knickers at all. My fingers were stained with pen and globs of glue. There were several empty Pot Noodles – Chicken and Mushroom flavour of course – and scattered tins of sweetcorn and Heinz tomato soup lining the thick windowsills. I was using the same fork and the same spoon for everything, and they lay, crusty, in the most recent tins I'd eaten straight out of. I realised then I hadn't had a poo in three days either – zero fruit and nothing but processed carbs will do that to you.

I hadn't quite made a noticeboard of clippings and ribbons all pointing towards the main suspect, waving my hands erratically with a fag hanging out my mouth as I explained my theories, but I'd done something quite close.

I presented to her: The Table. And, yes, I was gesticulating wildly, but I like to think it looked more like a clever magician revealing their tricks.

Everything I had found over the year of searching was spread out on the largest table in the room. I had cleared away the dusty boxes of crystal glasses and random pipes and scraps of notepads, and what was now in its place was my final piece. My science project, my display for the art show. A diorama of death, or something.

As if to add to the drama of the moment, the dark clouds broke around the distillery into a howling storm.

Morag remained half a metre or more away from me – out of disgust? I wasn't sure. I went to give her the tour anyway.

'Is this what I fucking think it is?' She gripped a nearby table for support and was rewarded with a hand covered in something sticky and dark. She almost went to rub it off on her trousers, before she reached over and rubbed her hand down on me instead. 'There. You're manky enough as it is.'

I thought of it as a minor concession. Morag was still being light-hearted, even while she vibrated with anger. I had learned by then that it was better to wait, let her sort herself and her thoughts out, before I jumped in with a joke to defuse the situation, which often had the opposite effect.

I stood as still as I could while adjusting the straps of my dungarees for comfort, as she walked around all sides of The Table.

Finally, she nodded and attempted an encouraging half-smile. Then she laughed and shook her head. 'For fuck's sake, Eilidh. I hope you're happy, because I am *absolutely raging*. But let's park that for now, because I am also very curious, of course I am. I always was, you know, but my brain only has space for so much. So, right, go on, you're dying to show off.'

'Okay, first let's start with – no, you need this to set the scene . . . or, actually, this might make more sense first–'

'How about I point at things and you splurge your brain out your mouth about them as I do?'

'Perfect, yes.' She's always known me so well.

'Right. I'm most interested in this shirt. I'm assuming, from the blood stains, this was somehow part of the original murder scene?'

'Yes, I found it hidden in a wall cavity in the toilet downstairs. I can only guess what she wore–'

'She?'

'Yes, I'm almost certain it was a woman.'

'I dunno, a lot of men wore quite fussy clothes in the seventies. Though, to be fair, it looks like something I might wear on a particularly dressy-feeling kind of day.'

'Well, maybe. You'll see why I say "she", just wait. So my guess is that maybe she stole a boilersuit from somewhere before she fled the scene. Either way, it makes sense she stashed it away. She whacks the guys, barrels them up, then cleans herself off. I've checked the label – it's polyester, which is why it hasn't deteriorated in all these years. It's from an old department store in Perth that doesn't exist anymore. Shut down about a decade ago. The label says it's a size twelve, but it looks tiny. Remember, whenever we buy vintage clothes, the sizes always come up small, don't they? Anyway, the sizing and the side that the buttons are on indicate it's a woman's blouse.'

'Sometimes people wear the clothes of the other gender,' Morag countered.

'Yes, but. Anyway, I'm not ashamed to say I've sniffed this all over.'

'Ahaha, of course you have. Right, let's get to it.' She didn't laugh.

'Well, I might have even given it a little sook and a lick in places. I'm sure it's what any good scientist would do.'

More disgust? No, her mouth was curling ever so slightly upwards. I was charming her, in my weird roundabout way. I continued. 'You see, it's definitely whisky in the stains here . . . and here. I'm not going to claim I'm so much of an expert that I could identify a whisky from the dried splotches on a shirt, but I can say for certain that that *is* whisky. And there's also a lot of blood.'

Morag leaned in and inhaled deeply into the largest yellow-brown splodge. She nodded. 'Okay, tell me about the . . . hair.'

One long strand of thick wavy red hair lay curled on top of a bright white sheet of paper.

'I found it in the barrel when I looked . . . that time. I

can't be sure it wasn't just on Duncan's jacket picked up from his daily life, but, look.'

I picked up the photograph of the woman talking in front of the crowd of men on the production floor. She had long, curly shining red hair, that proper orange kind, Merida from *Brave* kind.

Morag moved in closer to me. 'Do you think she did it? Who is she?'

'All in good time,' I said in my best Hercule Poirot impression, pretending to twiddle my moustache. 'What do you want to look at next?'

'The whisky. Why do you have all these bottles with washi tape on them?'

'I made those in secret. I started sampling the barrels from the years around 1971. There is a distinct improvement in the complexity of the flavours, how *smoothly* it goes down, post-1971, well, post-1974 or so. But only for a small handful of years.'

'Woah . . . really? And do you think these changes in the whisky have something to do with these . . . with the bodies?'

'Well. I managed to scour through lots of bits of papers – so disorganised and damaged – and in particular look at the master blender's weekly reports to the owner at the time. They were the most illuminating. Lots are missing, and most are written in an obnoxiously large, slanted cursive, the kind where the loops from the *g*s obscure the lines below, but I think I got the gist of it. Maybe you can help me decipher some more another time?' I pointed to the Post-it notes stuck here and there throughout the pile of papers, covered in words and question marks.

'Ah, so that's where my best Post-its went. I suspected it was you, since you're the only one I know who could make so much stuff disappear into the ether. I'm impressed – I haven't seen you create something so organised since your *Lost* obsession.'

'Aha, yes. I still love that show, but talk about plot abysses. Like Ben, he . . . Yes, sorry. Man, they did not hold back on their appraisals of their staff. Look. Here's Donald's dad – Hugh McLafferty.'

Morag picked up the paper and momentarily lifted her red-framed glasses onto her forehead to take a closer look. 'Wow, they called him "insufferably lazy"? And who uses the word "toerag" to describe an adult?'

We laughed together, and she followed this with, 'I reckon you're a little toerag, now I come to think of it. I've never thought about that word before – *toerag*. Do you think it means people had a specific cloth for wiping their toes?'

We giggled and shuddered gently into each other. Like we used to.

'Okay, and what about our be-tartaned twits? What of them?'

I flicked to two sheets of paper with thin blue labels sticking from the top and handed them to her to read.

The two fops came mincing in here late yet again, but they won't be reprimanded. One can't deny they get results. The most recent three distillations came in at nearly twenty

*per cent cheaper than this time last year, which you'll be
pleased about. I can't say I notice much difference on the
nose and palate, but the finish is harsher than we are used
to putting out. I doubt the customers will mind – they are
purchasing the name Ardkerran after all. They claim they
have simply tweaked the process somewhat, and if that's the
only difference I notice in the new make, then have at it, I
say. I'm sure you will agree – each bottle we sell will gain
us an additional £10 to £30.*

'Fops?' she questioned. 'Can they say that?'

'It was the seventies. I think most words were on the
table. Even in an official report. Although these reports feel
more like letters to a friend than business documents.'

'But are you sure it's Alistair and Duncan they're
referring to?'

I pointed to the second sheet; 'fop' is definitely the lesser
of the 'f' slurs used.

'Were they . . . together?'

'Aha, that brings me to my next piece of evidence,
madame!'

She looked at me, askance. 'Is this why you've been
watching David Suchet as Poirot this last month?'

'Yes, and Columbo before that. But my Columbo isn't
as charming. Ahh, one more question.' I mimed smoking
a cigar with my e-cigarette, blowing the kiwi-flavoured
vapour into the air. 'Take a quick look through these.'

'My, this is organised. Can you apply this approach to
our business a little more, hmm?'

Morag spent the next five minutes in near silence, apart from a little or large gasp here and there, as she read through the letters Sheena had found in the hole in the wall of the very room we were standing in. There was a blush forming on her cheeks and across her nose.

'This feels like reading the coded portions of Anne Lister's diaries!' she finally exclaimed, fanning herself. 'But again, can you be sure it's them? They're addressed to "CR" and "BB" or simply to "darling dearest".'

I shook my head but showed her a double spread in my notebook. It showed the dates of the letters matched against the dates of the distiller's reports.

'Some of the events match.' I used one of her pens to point at a paragraph. 'See here how "CR" mentions the rabbit covered in peat running through the malting floor and messing up his suit when he tried to catch it? The same thing is mentioned by the distiller, and he says it's Alistair's suit that was ruined by the peaty rabbit. There are a few other instances, but I'm certain "CR" is Alistair and "BB" is Duncan. What those initials stand for we can only guess. The other mysterious person . . .'

'Yes, the mysterious other.' I passed her a letter dated 11 July 1971. 'They seemed to have been in a sort of . . . throuple, if you look at this letter here.'

'Okay.' Morag nodded as she read, transfixed. 'They are mentioned several times.'

'And what pronouns are used?' I asked.

'She. Her. Hers. Wow. Is she the "she"? Do you think she did it? A crime of passion?'

'It points towards her. There were only two women working at the distillery at that time. And one of them, not long after these murders, rose through the ranks, you could say. This woman in particular, in the two photographs I found with Heather when I first brought her up here. It was Donald who identified her, remember?'

But she couldn't remember; she had blocked it out, using as much energy as possible to resist thinking of the men in barrels. Plus, she said, she was full of fear for me, after the accident at Hogmanay.

As we pieced together that short period of our lives, we somehow ended up in an embrace, talking only a centimetre away from each other's faces.

'I can't believe the time we lost. Maybe, maybe I should have just let you crack on with all of this. Maybe . . .'

I stared into her eyes, looking side to side into each one in turn, trying to memorise the flecks, the galaxies within them. Then I replied, quietly, 'No, Morag. I should have listened to you.'

We stood there like that for a moment more till the atmosphere between us became too intense; then we stepped apart, both wiping tears from our cheeks.

Realising I needed to change the emotional energy in the room, I swiftly jumped back towards the table, to distract us, to get this over and done with.

'Now, this is to move us onto the tasting portion of the event. You'll observe that it's a multi-sensory experience; you can't say I'm not good to you.'

I passed her two clean crystal tumblers, then poured a

little whisky from one of the bottles on the table into it.

'Eurgh, that's–' She coughed. 'Warn me next time!'

'It's more peppery than we're used to, that's for sure. Okay, now let's try one of these two – lady's choice.'

She elected the most amber of the three I gestured to. She smacked her lips after it went down.

'Wow . . . night and day. I mean, to me. It's still . . . smoky? But far easier on the gullet.'

'These three here are the same, give or take just a few short years, but then this one, this one is lacking the complexity, but by god, it's nowhere near as dark and crumbly as that first one. It's like the whisky was poor, then excellent, then the quality reduced once more. I wondered then, what was instigating that difference?'

Morag had followed me in my train of logic. 'The woman, the one who rose through the ranks or whatever you called it, was she high enough up in the distillery's hierarchy to yield such an influence?'

'Yes, she had "the best nose" they had come across, according to the reports.'

'So who is she? Is she still alive? Where is she now?'

'She's still alive and she lives here, in Campbeltown. Back then, she was called Julia Murray. But now she goes by–'

At precisely that moment the electricity shut off with a bang.

CHAPTER 35

You
2024

You're too old to do anything about the barrels now. There's still some strength left in these old bones but, well, osteoporosis is a real risk for women of your age. You'd always been so determined getting old wouldn't happen to you, but now it feels like nothing can stop the inexorable march of time.

You'd thought that perhaps befriending the new owners would help, that somehow you could stall or trick them, that that would keep your secret safe. As soon as the builders started bringing down the wall of the bottling room, perhaps that was when you knew there was no use. There was nothing you could do.

You've felt a strange affinity with them, those two lasses. You have a great affection for them. Everything you tried to do with Ardkerran all those years ago, they are doing. And so you've helped them.

Even the bottles. Those labels would have given the old guard a heart attack. And the cocktails they've made, even filmed for YouTube, that would have been sacrilege back in your day. Still is, to some people.

And now you know Eilidh has worked it out. The way she's been looking at you recently . . . like she's been re-evaluating everything about you. Maybe she's not quite there, but she soon will be.

She's been inviting you – well, not just you – but a group of you, to the distillery, to help her. It feels like an excuse to keep a closer eye on you.

You still know the hiding places, though, the ones your younger brother showed you when you were children. That's where you are now, when you hear Eilidh insist Morag follow her upstairs to the storage room, or whatever they are calling it now.

You creep up the stairs behind them.

You hear her say: 'I know who did it.'

You listen for long enough to know that she really has worked out it was you – at least, the Julia you – who did it.

You decide you might as well have some fun before it's all over. Before they officially connect the Julia you to you.

The fuses are where they have always been, and you laugh as you flick the large red one, pulling it down between both sets of fingers and thumbs.

CHAPTER 36

Eilidh
2024

We both screamed.

Then laughed, quietly, and found each other in the darkness.

We rubbed our heads into each other's shoulders and necks and arms and pulled close our warmth and love.

'Babe. Don't worry. Everything will be . . . groovy.'

We laughed again, louder this time. We both knew what it took for Morag to use that word, but it was exactly what we needed at that moment.

After all this time, all these renovations here, we felt like we knew every inch of the walls. After all, we put half of them there.

'Right, let's find those fuses.'

I wondered how many sentences in her life Morag has started with an emphatic *Right*. I was happy she was being decisive again. We needed at least one of us to be somewhat stable. We can't both fall apart and move through life unsure of ourselves. Even so, I think at that moment I was surer of myself than I had ever been.

Was it the storm that caused the blackout? I wondered. Then I realised that while we could kid ourselves, my gut instinct was too strong – someone was out there. Someone was listening to us.

Someone shut off the lights.

I pulled up the torch on my phone and swung it towards the area I thought the doorway was, so that we could leave, but instead of shining through into the piles of barley and kiln pipes, the beam lit up a body, a face, a person, standing there.

We were too shocked to scream again.

Bunty.

She looked . . . burning? Like her eyes were burning, like her body was firing up with an incandescent defiance.

I had to admit, it looked good on her.

'Well, girls, what's happened here?'

'Why don't you come in,' I said, 'and I'll show you. We can look together.'

'But first,' started Morag, 'let's get the lights back on?'

I glanced at her and saw that Morag looked relieved that Bunty had arrived, one of our pseudo grandparents.

I knew better.

'Why don't we all go to the fuses together? Bunty, you can lead the way.' She didn't look shocked at my suggestion. She was fiery but stoic. She knew I knew. She knew Morag hadn't pieced it together yet.

Morag was the only one talking, chattering away, barely audible above the crashing thunder every three minutes. I wondered what she was thinking then, was she curious at our silence?

Soon, lights back on, I led us back up to Aladdin's Cave. Back to the table of things, of clues, of the culmination of my year's work.

I didn't know what I was prouder of – establishing a working distillery or creating this.

'Well, Bunty,' I announced, 'I've pieced it together, mostly, and I know you know that. Can you illuminate Morag on the final piece of this mystery? And, actually, I am very nosy, as you are aware, so I want all the details, please. All the details of how you murdered Duncan and Alistair, and how you kept the truth about their deaths hidden for all these years.'

CHAPTER 37

You
2024

You are staring at a table of your life. Parts of your life. The photographs: you leading the charge on the newest batch of whisky; you all soft-focus in your tartan outfit, you and them outside these very gates, all those years ago. The familiar red *Campbeltown Courier* logo from all those decades ago, infinitesimally different than the one in the shops right now. The tea set you shared with Duncan. The clothes you wore when you murdered him and Alistair. You'd forgotten how much you loved frills back then. The lace is stiff with dark brown blood. You imagine it to be a tie-dye experiment, like you tried once with your mother, except the flakes that come off in between your crinkled and curled fingers as you rub the sleeves contradicts that notion.

Your fingers. Your hands. You turn them over and bring them towards you, almost grasping in your mind the image of what they once were: long, slim, pliable. Soft. Now they are hardened. Awkward. Old.

The time is now.

'It was me,' you say. 'These are my things. You found the bodies, I assume? Well, perhaps at some point you can tell me more about that. But, aye, it was me who killed them. Except I was Julia then. Julia Murray. Julia Charlotte Murray.'

Morag is frowning. She looks concerned, bewildered even, but Eilidh is burning with glee.

'I *knew* it was a woman – didn't I tell you, Morag? Didn't I say–'

'You said it *could* be a woman,' Morag corrects her, but now she's smiling, Eilidh's radiating energy seeping into her wife. The looks they share are something else. Open and beautiful. 'Shall I make us some tea then?'

You don't know where to start. They're not scared, not rushing to phone the police at any rate. You suppose, at seventy-six, you're not exactly a threat. You watch the candle's flame flicker, run your fingers round the rim of its hot glass jar. How does one condense fifty years and a lifetime of pain into a single tale? You feel a sort of vertigo just thinking about it, imagining the woman you were then, making tea in this very room, looking ahead and seeing you now.

'Do you . . . have any questions for me?'

Bruno potters in and leans his whole body against yours, looking up at you with a panting grin and eyes that melt. You scratch his neck, pat his ribs, rub his head. He jumps up onto the saggy, patched sofa, kicking off a flat cushion to cosy into you closer. He sighs.

Eilidh looks to Morag before she speaks. Morag gives a teeny nod, and the torrent begins.

'First of all, how the hell did you get them into those barrels? I mean, actually . . . first of all, why did you do it? Was it just you? Why are you called Bunty? I thought you said – didn't you say you only moved here twenty years ago or something? Okay – *why* did you kill Alistair and Duncan?'

'Actually,' I say, looking at them both in turn, 'I'd like to . . . if you'll permit me, it seems like it would make more sense if I start from the beginning.'

'Hang on a minute – I'll fetch the Hobnobs too. Let's settle in.'

As we wait for Morag to return, you can see Eilidh's mind whirring; her eyes dart and dance and flicker like the candlelight. She is appraising you. Reappraising you. You have grown awfully fond of her, of her and Morag together, the team they make, the balance in both, the lightness they bring to everyday things. She picks up a pen and starts writing something – you sip your tea and wait and observe.

'You know, I'd much prefer it if you don't record what I'm about to say.'

You startle her – she'd already shut off the world around her, descended entirely into her own.

'Ah, yes. I was actually making a mind map, of sorts, of clues I'm trying to connect together that didn't make sense before, and note some questions I still have, but . . . You're right. Best not to have this written down. Unless . . . can we burn it afterwards?'

You agree. Who are you to deny her this juicy delectable moment?

Morag returns with a tray. It's laden with some chicken treats for Bruno, a plate of Hobnobs, a jug of water, three tumblers and three bags of crisps, your favourite – ready salted.

'It's Sunday evening. The rain and thunder hasn't stopped for two days, and the sun has set. I think we can take our time this evening. Bunty – I mean, um, Julia?'

'Please, call me Bunty. That's who I am now.'

'Right,' Morag continues. 'We can set up the sofa for you to stay on tonight, if you'd like?'

'Yes, please, I'd like that very much. Let's wait to see what you think of me after this conversation, though. Shall I begin?'

You pause and take in the room. The artwork they've added. The cosiness of the place. It was pure business back when you were in here last. It is time to begin.

'Ardkerran was my playground. On the way to school, which was in town, my brothers and I would stop to shout to our dad – he was often in the yard outside, moving barrels and the like. The smell. No matter where I've been in the world, the sweet yeasty smell of a distillery draws me in. I was the adventurous one, out of us three. Of course, I was also the girl, and the youngest, but if anything that's why I was the way I was. Maybe I felt like I had something to prove. Anyway, sometimes we wouldn't go to school, and I was usually the instigator.

'In those days, really, as long as you were helping

and not a hindrance, they didn't mind a helping hand. Jonathan slunk about with the distillery's cat, climbing around the eaves and all kinds of nooks and crannies most of the adults would never know were there, catching rats.'

Bruno lifts his head expectantly, whether at the word 'rats' or at the women's small, disgusted scoffs at the word. You settle him with a stroke and sip your tea.

'I helped with the malting. It was tough work, but I remember . . . I can still picture the moment one of the men snapped off the top half of a rake so I could manage it better. That was mine, now. Our mum would sniff us when we got home, test us on what we'd learned at school that day, test our father when he got home and all. He was proud, I think . . . proud that we were already so ingrained with the lifeblood of our community. He wasn't an educated man – I don't think Mum was either. But they were sharp, sharp as hell. Dad knew we were learning more there than we might at school. Besides, it wasn't like I was expected to get a job; my job was just to find a man and settle down, become a mother. Ha!'

'Aye, not much has changed in that department. But when was that? And what about Alistair and Duncan?' Eilidh most definitely wants you to speed it up a bit, but she doesn't want to be rude. She can wait. You're savouring this. You've waited for this. You almost hoped it would come eventually, no matter the consequences.

'Okay, I knew from a young age that's where I wanted to be. At the distillery. I wanted to do what my dad did

– I didn't want to do what my mum did. But there was only one woman who worked for the distillery then, and she was the secretary – I suppose that's what you could call her. Elspeth was her name. Always made time for me. I'd learned the systems and secrets of that place by the time I was fourteen. Plus, I'd take any job she'd give me – I did a lot of licking of stamps, let me tell you. I can still taste them. So the only way I knew that would allow me to stay a part of the distillery, as a woman, was to work in the office. Most days would involve trips downstairs, usually to berate someone for not filling something out properly. Elspeth, she had this . . . power. Then, when I was about twenty, she got engaged. I didn't understand at the time, it didn't make sense to me, but she kept saying it "wasn't the done thing" for a married woman to continue working. That was probably the seed that grew in me – *I'm never getting married then*, that's what I used to think. And so I took her job.

'Alistair and Duncan were both about ten years older than me. There was always something about them that differentiated them from the other men. It was like they had this tenderness. It was an open secret, something joked about yet mostly accepted, that they were quite camp really. "Flamboyant" was one of the kinder terms, but they took all the jibes and slurs in their stride. It was mostly harmless, and it never changed them. They were one of us, part of Campbeltown. Or so I thought.

'The relationship between us three began innocently enough. Duncan often spent time up here – I've always loved reading, you see, and he'd joke about the others not knowing their Byron from their backside. We'd drink tea – like we are now – except out of that darling patterned teapot and matching teacups and saucers. We reserved it just for us.

'One afternoon, Alistair came upstairs, so flustered – I'd never seen him so flustered – and perhaps it was because Duncan was so comfortable with me, or because Alistair was so distressed, but he grabbed him and held him, kissed his face and head all over. I think they forgot I was there, because suddenly they sprang apart. Being gay – having gay sex – was illegal then, you know, at least in Scotland, right up until 1980. That was one thing England was ahead of us for, at the time.'

Morag squeezes Eilidh's hand. You feel a pang of jealousy – what could your life have been like if you could have chosen to spend it as they have? If you'd had an option to love whomever you wanted to, openly?

You shake your head. You know life's not been easy or kind for the young ones either. Plus you had your adventures.

'Well . . . they both blushed. I stepped up to hug them and we cried together, embraced like that for a while. It felt good to be part of their secret, to know that there were at least two people on this peninsula living how they wanted. At least to an extent. Of course, it had to be hidden from the world at large.'

'Then . . .' You can't explain the next bit. It hurts.

'You don't need to tell us everything, you know. I know Eilidh wants all the details, but just . . . whatever you're comfortable with,' Morag says, as Eilidh nods, somewhat unconvincingly.

'Okay then, yes, thank you. Essentially, after that, I started up a relationship with Duncan. Sort of like Duncan was my boyfriend and Alistair was his. We'd often, you know . . .' You decide euphemisms don't suit you. 'Have sex. The three of us. It worked. I think I was more aware of it having a shelf life than they were, but we got caught up in it, you know?

'I was so alive; life was so full. It was like we never had an end to our conversations. We had so many threads going at once, and no matter whether we appeared to begin a thought apropos of nothing, or a week had passed since we last discussed it, we each knew which thread to follow. And then . . .'

Eilidh stops mid-crunch. Morag holds her tea halfway to her mouth. Bruno pats me with his paw so that I resume my strokes.

'I found out the bastards were putting out vast quantities of poor product.'

Eilidh coughs on her Hobnob. Morag slams her mug onto the table and liquid slops onto the already very stained wood. Bruno grunts.

'I think you of all people could understand exactly how betrayed I felt. Like all our conversations, all our shared passion for whisky, for Ardkerran, for Campbeltown, meant nothing.'

Eilidh has been quiet and patient for a while now, so you let her speak.

'Oh. My. God. But they knew that was a key reason why all but a couple of Campbeltown distilleries shut down in the 1920s? They knew that even one batch could ruin the reputation of, of, of . . . not just your distillery, but the whole area! How poor are we talking? We tried some, and I thought there was a difference! I mean, not that I doubt you but, um, couldn't you have done something about it? Couldn't you change it, hide it, work things out, reason with them? What about the others? Oh my gosh, how long for? How did they get away with it? What–' Morag stops her with a pat on the hand. 'Sorry, please carry on.'

'I knew you'd understand. I am cognisant of the fact that, perhaps, this "poor product" did not merit their, hmm, end. I can only say I wasn't quite myself.

'It was the final night of production for that year before the season of cleaning began. We'd all been out celebrating, and the three of us had sneaked back to the distillery, eager to, well, you know, *shag*, in the warehouse, while it was empty. Even the two security guards were out at the pub that night. It was a fun idea. A dangerous idea.

'I insisted we take a nip of the new make ourselves. Maybe they didn't think I'd a good enough nose to know, but I did. I bloody well did. I could tell something was off; in my gut, I could feel they were acting strange. They laughed – can you believe this – they laughed as they told me all the corners they'd cut to push this batch out. Butts of the stuff, they said.'

'But why? Why would they do that? Duncan especially was known for being a legendary blender, right? They both grew up here, too, didn't they? Why would they just—'

Morag cuts her off again. 'Money. Aye?'

'Aye,' you say. 'They'd stupidly accepted huge orders with tight deadlines from large drinks companies who wanted our whisky for blending; they didn't see the bigger picture like I did. They thought they could continue like that for a while – had even projected forwards for the next five years. They were arrogant. Alistair was convinced your average person – and the people at these drinks companies – wouldn't be able to tell, that the subtle delicacies of whisky were beyond them. I knew better. Plus, I could tell from their attitude they felt that they actually didn't owe the company anything. They wanted to take the money and run, essentially.

'So I—'

'Killed them,' Morag and Eilidh chime in unison.

'Yes. I had to stop them. I was so angry I grabbed this massive iron tool and whacked Duncan in the side of the head. That was all it took. Alistair fell to the floor immediately. He was holding his hands in front of me, pleading, but I couldn't stop myself and I hit him too – it took three hard blows for him. I felt so heartbroken, so deeply betrayed, that I lashed out. They had no remorse, you see; they didn't care about the town, about the whisky, about any of it anymore. They just laughed when they told me they had no desire to go back to making good whisky. Money had blinded them, just as my rage blinded me that night.

'In that moment I did what I thought was sensible – I pulled out the bungs and emptied two butts. I think it took me an hour, maybe two, to work up the courage to actually put them in the barrels. Enough to finish off half a seventy cl of our signature blend, anyhow.

'I shouldn't have waited though. They were starting to stiffen. I had to crack and shove and pull.'

Your eyes are wide now. You can see the scene more clearly than you have ever before – the memory you've pushed away for so long is playing out in technicolour in front of you.

'I refilled their barrels to the brim, hammered the lids back in and rolled them, with some difficulty, I might add, to the back of the warehouse. I cleaned, I wiped, and then I ran. I had planned to, I don't know, roll the barrels into the sea or something.'

You aren't sure how to continue. How did it work out for you for so long? So much luck, so much in your favour. You came to learn that, despite how integral they were to operations, how outwardly fond others seemed of them, life moved on very quickly.

They are silent now, but with vastly different looks on their faces. Morag keeps starting to speak, then looking between you and Eilidh.

'Yes?' you say.

She turns to Eilidh and says quietly, 'I can see you understand more than I do, but . . . Eilidh, are you not . . . should we not feel . . . these men were two of ours . . .'

'She didn't kill them because they were gay,' Eilidh states.

Morag still seems conflicted, but she turns to you again.

'But why did no one look for them?' she says. 'They can't have found their bodies, so why weren't they searched for?'

Eilidh answers for you. 'They had a boat, didn't they? It was found with the wheel broken. Alcohol on board. It was presumed to be a drowning. What did you do?'

'Yes. I decided to tamper with the boat in the hope that the police would search there instead. We did search for them. For two days. They even sent boats out around the loch, but they never found them – of course they didn't – but the police weren't fussed about two poofs going missing. They said that – they actually said that themselves. And there were other men who'd wanted to move up the ranks in the distillery for a while – and it was, well, is again, one of the main employers here. Two more jobs to go round.'

You have never told anyone this. You always thought it would be to the police if you did. Not like this. Although the longer time went on, the less likely it seemed it would happen.

'Can I ask . . .' Eilidh began.

You nod, hoping it is a question you can answer, hoping, even after all of this, that, somehow, they will still like you.

'Did you start the fire on Hogmanay?'

Shame, hot shame, burning harsher than the decades' old guilt of murder, floods your body.

'Yes,' you reply. 'I didn't want anyone to get hurt. You just got caught in the cross-fire. I was trying . . . I wasn't thinking . . . I wanted the bodies to be gone.'

You try to ascertain what Morag and Eilidh are thinking. To determine what happens next.

CHAPTER 38

Eilidh

2027

Our first official Scottish whisky is here – gleaming. After three years and a day of maturation, our product stands in neat rows of bottles behind the bar of the visitor centre. Donald has a case ready to go in his pub too.

Morag is in her element – this is really what she's been waiting for. All the renovations, all the big jobs, she has enjoyed the co-ordination of those. But here, the finicky bits, the final touches, the hosting – this is what she thrives on. I watch her zip back and forth, in the midst of short, sharp and practically one-sided conversations, keeping the phone in her hand for instant access in case she has a sudden thought or a call comes through.

There's already a gaggle of visitors at the gates, waiting. Mostly locals, but a few hardcore whisky enthusiasts too, wanting to say they were here first. I spot Heather, Zahir and Gordon there too, and a couple of other journalist types. A warm jolt shakes through me when I pick out other familiar faces – Susan, Lillian, Morag's parents, Sheena et al. I wish Winnie was still alive to see this, so she could see what she has wrought through me.

The clock says it is only half past eight, and I am happy not to rush Morag. The crowd outside can wait.

I enjoy probably the earliest dram I've ever had – if you don't count the nights I continued on into the wee hours. I take one sip per minute, savouring.

At 8.57 a.m., Morag approaches me. 'Are you ready? Shall we open a little early? Get the ribbon cutting over and done with and crack on with our very first tour?'

I reply with a deep malty kiss.

Our tour starts with a little history video, as many of these distillery tours do. As I observe the crowd watching the screen, I lean on two heavily lacquered sherry butts that form part of the scenery. They have jars of barley and grist atop, and stuffed hessian sacks around them. Only three people still alive know what is inside those barrels.

ACKNOWLEDGEMENTS

My first acknowledgement goes to my husband, Ross. You have kept me well fed, reminded me to shower, and given me so much love and cheerleading, and many grounding, bone-breaking hugs at the end of long days. I also want to thank Mira, Hannah and Georgie – we speak every day, and I cannot measure how much your wisdom, humour and care mean to me. Thank you to Mum for surrounding me with books and love and encouraging me to write from a young age, to Dad for keeping me topped up in coffee syrups to power my writing, and to my sister Claudia, who has exactly the same sense of humour as me and kindly read several early versions of this novel. Similarly to Stephen Ross – thank you for reading my different drafts and being such a helpful sounding board, and to Paula Gludovatz who gave very thorough comments.

I want to thank Bloody Scotland for selecting my 100-word pitch to present this novel idea and the panel for their helpful comments on the day – and especially to Jenny Brown who creates such wonderful experiences for new authors and is now my very own agent! A big thank you to Kaite Welsh who helped me edit my pitch and strongly encouraged I keep within the allotted time. Thank you also to Fiona Brownlee who saw my pitch and enthusiastically recommended me to Alison Rae, Senior Editor at Polygon. I won the golden ticket when I gained such an experienced editor who not only has so much insight but understood my vision. Thank you too to Emma Hargrave who gave superb feedback in the initial edits and helped me see the wood for the trees.

To our Shelf Satisfaction book group – no matter how awesome or terrible that month's book is, however much we have actually read of the book, we always have such a laugh. Thank you to all of you who read some/all/none of my drafts of this novel – being in a safe space to share my work and ideas is something I will always cherish.

My writing journey began in earnest in 2020, when Kevin P. Gilday offered free spoken word workshops and created The Scribbler's Union. He encouraged me to perform and to embrace my energetic style, and the next stage of my life began. I wouldn't be confident on stage otherwise, or have given myself a real shot at trying a writing career. My editor at SNACK Magazine, Kenny Lavelle, has trusted me with so much and given me the feedback that has most impacted my writing, especially how to say more with less. Thank you to Alan McMunnigall at Thi Wurd and everyone in the writing group – all your advice, thoughts and questions are always so compassionate and helpful and give me new perspective on my writing.

To James Ley and all the Earlybird Pomodoro writers – I can't believe that it has been years now that we have been meeting at 7 a.m. on Zoom. It enabled me to write this novel plus a great many other things – and all of your sage and grounded advice has been invaluable in my writing journey.

Finally, a big thank you to the Campbeltown Heritage Centre, who opened up just for me one blustery October morning and offered a wealth of local knowledge and tales.